D0338868

STORIES AND MIRACLES
OF
OUR LADY
OF GOOD SUCCESS

by

Marian Therese Horvat, Ph.D.

4

Copyright © 2002 by Marian Therese Horvat

First edition by TIA, Inc. 2002.
Second edition by TIA, Inc. in 2006.
Third edition by TIA, Inc. in 2011.

All rights reserved. No part of this booklet may be reproduced
or transmitted in any form or by any means whatsoever, including the Internet, without permission in writing from the au-
thor, except that brief selections may be quoted or copied for
non-profit use without permission, provided full credit is given.

ISBN: 0-9672166-7-2
Library of Congress Number: 2002090207
Printed and bound in the United States of America

Cover: Statue of Our Lady of Good Success, Quito, Ecuador.

TRADITION IN ACTION, INC.
P.O. Box 23135
Los Angeles, CA 90023
Phone: 323-725-0219
Fax: 323-725-0019
www.TraditionInAction.org

TABLE OF CONTENTS

FOREWORD

The book *Stories and Miracles of Our Lady of Good Success* by Marian Therese Horvat, as well as her prior work *Our Lady Of Good Success – Prophecies for Our Times,* show that the messages contained in the revelations of Our Lady of Good Success and of Our Lady of Fatima are sister messages. Both warn us of a crisis of world proportion that affected the Holy Catholic Church in the 20th century. Both stimulate us to the fight for the threatened Faith, to prayer, and to sacrifice. Both promise us a restoration of the Church and Christendom under the salutary protection of the Blessed Virgin.

The fact that three hundred years prior to the 20th century, Our Lady had pointed to the present-day crisis in the Church expresses the magnitude of this calamity. From a great distance one can see only the gigantic mountains.

And what is the crisis that has affected the entire Church in the 20th century?

The only phenomenon that occurred in the 20th century with a dimension proportional to the forewarnings of Our Lady of Good Success and that changed the face of the Catholic Church was the Ecumenical Council of Vatican II.

This statement is confirmed by the opinion that the unrevealed part of the message of Fatima is a warning that relates to this Council. Various Cardinals and important theologians specializing in Mariology have held this opinion from Pius XII until today. The present Vatican, however, by means of two important Cardinals of the Curia, Cardinal Angelo Sodano, Secretary of State, and Cardinal Joseph Ratzinger, Prefect of the Congregation for the Doctrine of the Faith, entered the scene to try to silence this opinion.

The two Cardinals released a letter in 2000 that was supposedly the entire text of the unrevealed part of the Fatima message. The text does not fit with the ensemble of the prior revelations. It does not mention the main point that was expected: the *cause* of the crisis that affects the Church and the world. The two Cardinals, however, tried to impose that there is nothing more to say about the prophecies of Fatima.

It is not the custom for the Church to give official interpretations of private prophecies. Normally the Holy See judges if a prophecy of this type has something against Faith and Morals. It either does or does not. If it does not have anything against Faith and Morals, the interpretations of the messages are free and open to discussion. The two Cardinals, however, broke with this custom of the Holy See, and came out publicly trying to impose a certain interpretation – which in itself, by the way, is entirely disputable. They did this, as far as I can see, to silence the message of Fatima in its anti-progressivist and anti-ecumenical character. They also implicitly denied the threat of a chastisement of world proportions followed by the promise of a new era of glory for the Church. It is understandable that the present day Vatican, infiltrated by all kinds of progressivist ideas, would not be comfortable with the message of Fatima and would attempt a maneuver of this sort.

The maneuver, however, has not been successful. This "official burying" of the Fatima message by the two Cardinals has not satisfied the faithful. The majority is still waiting for something else. But it is almost certain that nothing different from the latest letter and interpretation of Fatima will be forthcoming from the Vatican.

In this perplexing situation, a new factor has appeared on the horizon, unexpected, like all truly prophetic actions. "The prophetic action is a surprise from God," says a popular adage. It applies in this case. The two Cardinals pulled the tablecloth too far to one side of the table in their effort to cover the message of Fatima. The result is that the other side of the table was left exposed. What has appeared is the providential message of the prophecies of Our Lady of Good Success that deal with the same crisis. These prophecies are even clearer than Fatima about the cause of the present crisis in the Holy Church.

I believe that when Marian T. Horvat published her first book in 1999, she could not have imagined the benefit it would give the Church by beginning to spread the message of Our

Lady of Good Success. The book that today comes to light, *Stories and Miracles of Our Lady of Good Success*, confirms and fortifies the message of the first book.

The stories in this book are beneficial also for other reasons. They help to spread devotion to Our Lady of Good Success, as she herself foretold would happen. They transmit to the reader the charming ambience of grace and intimacy with the Mother of God. An ambience that existed in that blessed Convent of the 17th century and that promises to be restored in the future for all of mankind.

This is a book with a prophetic message, with something of the *Golden Legend* and something of a book of piety.

After reading it, one wants to know even more.

Atila Sinke Guimarães

Los Angeles, February 2, 2002
Feast day of Our Lady of Good Success

Two views of the Conceptionist Church and Convent on the corner of the downtown plaza in Quito, Ecuador.

INTRODUCTION

It is a great consolation for me to write about Our Lady of Good Success. I have loved her since I first learned of this invocation. I read whatever I could find about the apparitions and Mother Mariana de Jesus Torres, and made two pilgrimages to Ecuador to see the miraculous statue of Our Lady of Good Success. It is really impossible to describe the majesty, maternal goodness, and celestial intimacy that permeate the sacred statue. Even the best pictures do not transmit the supernatural presence and beauty that one experiences at the feet of Our Lady there.

I made a promise to divulge what I could about this devotion before the end of the 20th century, since Our Lady explicitly said that she would become known under this invocation at this time. It was only in 1999 that the opportunity came for me to publish a short book.[1] Now, in 2002, I return to the same subject.

In the first book, I presented a summary of the main facts related to this blessed invocation. I had, however, to choose among the many "successes" that pertain to the stories of the miraculous statue and the life of Madre Mariana de Jesus Torres. I chose to concentrate on the major prophecies of Our Lady of Good Success that refer to our difficult times. There were many details that I could not include in the short work, but I had the hope of reporting them at some later time, when Our Lady would indicate the right moment to do so.

The good reception of the first book, the spontaneous reaction of many readers asking for more details, and the encouragement of some close friends led me to write this second one. In it I will deal with details surrounding the making of the statue, as well as relate several stories and miracles that took place during the life of Mother Mariana.

There are still many other stories to relate from the life of Mother Mariana based on the Spanish documents I translated,

---

[1] Marian Therese Horvat, *Our Lady of Good Success – Prophecies for Our Times* (Los Angeles: TIA, Inc., 1999).

in particular, the 1790 work of Friar Manuel Souza Pereira,[2] who died in the odor of sanctity. I hope that a third book in the future will bring these to light.

*

Here let me remind the reader of some points from the first book.

The protagonist is Venerable Mother Mariana de Jesus Torres, a Conceptionist religious who traveled from Spain to the Royal Colony of Quito, Ecuador in 1576 to play a providential role for Quito and the world. During her lifetime, by means of numerous revelations, she was given to see and know many important events of the future,

The main revelation she received regarded the great crisis that would afflict the Church throughout the 20th century, and especially the last half. Our Lady of Good Success told her that in our lamentable times, heresies would abound, the corruption of manners and customs would be almost complete, religious vocations would decline, and the light of the Faith nearly extinguished. To atone for the many profanities, blasphemies, and abuses and to hasten the day of the triumphant restoration, this 17th century religious was asked to become an expiatory victim for our times. Thus, in a special way, the vocation of Mother Mariana links her to us and to our days.

Our Lady of Good Success, like Our Lady of Fatima, foresaw not only a terrible crisis, but also a great restoration of the Catholic Church and Christendom. These were her words to Mother Mariana: "To be delivered from the slavery of these heresies [of the 20th century], those whom the merciful love of my Son has destined for this restoration will need great will power, perseverance, courage, and confidence in God. To try the faith and trust of these just ones, there will be times when all

---

[2] *The Admirable Life of Mother Mariana of Jesus Torres, a Spaniard and One of the Foundresses of the Royal Convent of the Immaculate Conception of the City of Saint Francis of Quito*, English translation by Marian T. Horvat, Copyright 1999, unpublished.

will seem lost and paralyzed. This will be the happy beginning of the complete restoration."

The devotion of Our Lady of Good Success in Quito was born in 1610. In several apparitions, Our Lady instructed Mother Mariana to have a life-size statue of her made under the invocation of Our Lady of Good Success. She told her to make it exactly as she appeared to her, with the crosier and the keys to the cloister in her right hand, and her Divine Child on her left arm. This would be "so that men will understand how powerful I am in placating the Divine Justice and in obtaining mercy and pardon for every sinner who comes to me with a contrite heart, for I am the Mother of Mercy and in me there is only goodness and love. Let them come to me, for I will lead them to Him." The statue, made by a sculptor in Quito, was miraculously completed by the Archangels Michael, Gabriel, and Raphael in the early morning of January 16, 1611.

I hope this brief summary will help the reader understand what he will read here.

*

Finally, there are several clarifications I would like to make.

My first book, whose primary emphasis was on the prophecies of Our Lady of Good Success, summarized many facts related to the apparitions and the life of Mother Mariana de Jesus Torres. In this second book I will deal with some of the same episodes, but with much greater detail. It is inevitable, therefore, that there will be some repetition in order to give the reader the complete picture. As far as possible, however, I will avoid repetition and will simply indicate in footnotes the places in *Our Lady of Good Success: Prophecies for Our Times* where the topic is presented.[3]

---

[3] The pages cited will be from the 2nd edition of *Our Lady of Good success: Prophecies for our Times* (Los Angeles: TIA, Inc, 2000).

The sequence of facts in the book can be confusing at times to the reader who likes a strict chronological presentation of events. To give him a comfortable portrait of the ensemble, at the end of this book is a chronology of the landmark events related in both books that can situate the reader in the 16th and 17th centuries, when the apparitions of Our Lady took place.

The title of Founding Mother was reserved for the seven religious who traveled from Spain to Ecuador to establish the Royal Convent of the Immaculate Conception. It was a title of respect, and did not imply *per se* an authority. Mother Maria Taboada, the first Abbess, was elected by the other sisters, and in accordance with the Convent Rule, a new election was held every three years. Mother Mariana, who succeeded her aunt in government, held the office of Abbess various times in her life. The five remaining Founding Mothers, who held different offices in the Convent, formed a kind of organic counsel to advise Mother Mariana, but the title conferred no juridical power.

The statue of the Divine Infant we see today in the arms of Our Lady of Good Success is not the original statue. The original, according to descriptions of the time, was the worthy match of the perfect and majestic statue of Our Lady. During a revolution, a sister hid the statue of the Infant along with some important documents from the Convent archives in a wall of the building. The religious died a short time afterward without revealing the location where the objects were hidden. To replace the lost one, another statue of the Child was made, which does not achieve the same perfection as the first. According to a prophecy made to Mother Mariana, the original statue will be found, but only after the present crisis has ended and the restoration of the Holy Church has begun.

*   *   *

Our Lady of Good Success in her niche in the upper choir
of the cloister where she governs and protects the
Convent until the end of time.

Mother Mariana held one end of the cord, while Our Lady took the other and brought it to her forehead. The cord stretched miraculously to the exact height of the Virgin Mary as she appeared to Mother Mariana. The painting commemorating the event hangs in the Conceptionist Church in Quito.

Chapter I

A BRIEF REVIEW OF THE LIFE OF MOTHER MARIANA DE JESUS TORRES (1563-1635)

Born in the province of Biscay, Spain, Mariana Francisca de Jesus Torres y Berriochoa left her home at age 13 to help found a Conceptionist Convent in the Spanish Colony of Quito. From the very beginning, the devil tried to impede the founding of this Convent in the New World. Soon after they embarked, the small group was beset by a great tempest that threatened to sink their ship. Mariana was given to see a monstrous seven-headed serpent in the waters that was threatening to sink the ship to prevent the Convent from being established. In the vision she had during the storm, the serpent was vanquished by the Holy Virgin carrying the Child Jesus in her left arm. At the same time she understood the providential role that God had destined for this Convent.

Under the sure guidance of her holy aunt, Mother Maria de Taboada, the novice Mariana grew in holiness and virtue, and in 1579 made the solemn profession of her religious vows. Embracing a life of severe penance and constant prayer, she was often the recipient of mystical favors and heavenly visions. The life of Mariana de Jesus Torres was also a succession of great sufferings and terrible persecutions, even within the Convent she had helped to found. After having been elected Abbess, she was unjustly imprisoned four times by rebellious native sisters of Quito, who were seeking to relax the rule and to remove the Convent from the direction of the Franciscans to the Diocese.[4] Divine Providence asked Mother Mariana to suffer the torments of Hell for five years as an expiatory victim for the conversion of the leader of these rebellious sisters so that she might escape eternal damnation. She heroically accepted this hard sentence for the sister who had been her chief tormenter.

---

[4] See *Our Lady of Good Success: Prophecies for Our Times*, Chap. II.

One of the most extraordinary facts in the life of Mother Mariana is that of her three deaths. The Convent's archival evidence documents that this holy religious died in 1582 and returned to life. She suffered a second death on Good Friday of 1588 and was resurrected two days later at dawn on Easter Sunday. Finally, in her third and last death, she ended her earthly exile on January 16, 1635.

The apparitions of Our Lady of Good Success have received diocesan approval since their origins in the early 17th century. At the command of her superiors, Mother Mariana left a full account of her life, which was approved by the Most Rev. Pedro de Oviedo, Quito's tenth Bishop, who personally knew and directed the holy Conceptionist religious.

Her first biography was written by her last confessor and spiritual director, Fr. Michael Romero, O.F.M. Based on these documents, Franciscan Friar Ochoa de Alacano published a work that spread widely in the Franciscan monasteries in the Old and New Worlds. It was reading this work that began the conversion of a young Portuguese military officer who in 1777 became a priest, Fr. Manuel Souza Pereira. Fr. Pereira later traveled to the New World and became the spiritual director of the Conceptionist religious of Quito. At their request, he wrote a work titled *The Admirable Life of Mother Mariana of Jesus Torres*, and it is upon his long and detailed account that this work is largely based.

In several apparitions, the Virgin Mary asked Mother Mariana to have a statue made in honor of her under the invocation of Our Lady of Good Success. The next chapters will give many details about this miraculous undertaking so rich in implications for our days.

The statue continues to be venerated in the Conceptionist Convent in Quito today with full diocesan approval.[5]

---

[5] Msgr. Luis E. Cadena Y Almeida, postulator of the cause of beatification of the Servant of God, Mother Mariana de Jesus Torres, has written three books on the topic: one on the life of Mother Mariana, another on the origins of the cult to the Blessed Virgin of Good Success, and

Three times a year, it leaves the Abbess' seat and is displayed for public veneration, which continues to grow. For Our Lady herself told Mother Mariana that the story of the statue's origin and Mother Mariana's life would become known at the end of the 20th century, and she is keeping her word.

* * *

---

another (unpublished) on the prophetic messages that time has verified as true.

The statue is placed on the altar of the Church for public veneration for nine days before and after the Feast day of the Purification of the Blessed Virgin, February 2, and during the months of May and October.

Chapter II

A COMMAND FOR A STATUE TO BE MADE

The story of a saint is always the story of the way of the cross. God wants his creatures to be tested. The infinite seriousness of God demands a proof of man's love, a holocaust. There is nothing more fecund than the holocaust man offers by embracing the sacrifice of self for the love of God. Once offered and made, something is born destined to give good fruit. Today there are persons so averse to suffering they cannot understand the role it plays in forming truly grand souls. But Our Lady always has her chosen souls, like Mother Mariana de Jesus Torres, to whom she gives this understanding. It is her custom to prepare such souls to accept and even embrace the Way of the Cross; at the same time, she consoles them with her favors and smiles.

Mother Mariana de Jesus Torres was no stranger to the cross. The penances and sufferings she voluntarily embraced during her religious life seem almost incomprehensible to the modern mindset. After her first death in 1582, she appeared before the Divine Tribunal and was judged guiltless. Our Lord presented her with two crowns: one, a heavenly crown that she could receive immediately, and another, of lilies with sharp thorns that she would have to wear for some time longer on earth. She chose the latter and returned to earth for 53 more years to suffer and to offer herself as an expiatory victim for our own times.[6]

In this Convent that cost so much sacrifice and prayer, she and the five other Founding Mothers[7] were persecuted and

---

[6] Ibid., pp. 27-8.

[7] The names of these holy Mothers deserve mention, for they, along with Mother Mariana, were the pillars of this Convent destined by God to last until the end of the earth. These religious, who all adhered strictly to the observance of the Rule and lived lives of prayer and sacrifice, were Mothers Francisca of the Angels, Anne of the Conception, Lucia of the Cross, Magdalena of St. John, Catherine of the Conception, and Maria of the Incarnation. One of the prophecies Our Lady

imprisoned four times by rebellious and jealous native sisters. At times, when the other Founding Mothers protested and could not understand how she could bear so much ingratitude and slander from the rebellious sisters, Mother Mariana de Jesus Torres replied: "Since it is those who persecute us who are forming our souls for Heaven, let us love them dearly. For, if the beautiful statues had the use of reason, they would dearly love the instruments that carved and polished them. We, then, who have the use of reason, should do what the statues cannot do."

Our Lady showed Mother Mariana how much this willingness to bear with the ingratitude of her sisters and to suffer valorously for their conversion pleased Our Lord. During the third imprisonment of Mother Mariana and the other Founding Mothers in January of 1582, the Abbess received a great favor from Heaven and the weighty charge to have a statue of Our Lady made under the invocation of Our Lady of Good Success.

Messengers from Heaven

At midnight on January 16, 1599, Mother Mariana, as was her custom, rose to pray and to beg divine mercy upon her beloved Convent in this lamentable period. For the infernal spirit had seized control of the native sisters to try to subvert the order and finally destroy the motherhouse of the Order of the Immaculate Conception in Ecuador. He inflamed them with a jealousy against the Spanish Founding Mothers, whom they maligned with calumnies and accused of demanding too great rigor in the observance of the Rule.

At one in the morning, she heard a melodious voice accompanied by a zither, and the prison became illuminated with a celestial light. Suddenly she saw before her the Seraphic St.

---

revealed to Mother Mariana was that in the happy days of the restoration, the Convent would again have sisters with these names, and that each one would found a daughter branch. The perfectly incorrupt bodies of Mother Mariana and the other Founding Mothers are all preserved in the cloisters of the Conceptionist Convent in Quito.

Francis, playing the zither, and the recently deceased first Founding Abbess, Mother Maria de Jesus Taboada, who intoned couplets of mournful love. Mother Mariana was transported with joy and a longing to join the celestial happiness of her aunt, who addressed her with these words:

"My daughter and niece, never have you been so pleasing to Our Lord as during this present time, when sorrow engulfs you. Ah! If you only knew the value of suffering unjustly for love of monastic observance! To recompense your constancy and your humble suffering, my Seraphic Father and I have come to delight your ears and fill your heart with celestial consolation."

Then St. Francis spoke, "Take courage and remain steadfast in practicing monastic observance, for the rewards in Heaven that await the observant religious are great. Whoever loves me and follows my spirit will be loved and blessed by God, and whoever swerves from my spirit, I will neither recognize nor defend before the Supreme Tribunal. This Convent, so beloved by me, will be privileged. I will watch unceasingly over it until the end of time, for in all centuries it will have some faithful and loving daughters. Now, expand your heart and prepare yourself, for our Sovereign and Queen is coming to visit your prison. We are only her messengers."

The First Visit of Our Lady of Good Success

Then, in a light more brilliant than that which surrounded St. Francis and Mother Maria Taboada, Our Lady appeared carrying the Divine Infant in her left arm and a crosier in her right hand. On the crosier was a cross of diamonds, each one shining like the sun. In the middle of the cross was a ruby star engraved with the name of Mary, which radiated many lights, each one more brilliant than the last.

"I am Mary of Good Success," she told the humble religious, "your Mother from Heaven, to whom you always resort under this invocation so well known in Spain …. The tribulations that my Most Holy Son has given you are a celestial gift by which your souls may embellish themselves and hold back His divine ire, so ready to unleash a terrible chastisement upon this ungrateful Colony. How many hidden crimes are committed in this city and the surrounding area! For precisely this reason, this Convent was founded here so that the God of Heaven and Earth would be avenged in the very place where He is offended and unrecognized. For this reason also, the demon, enemy of God and of the just, both now as well as in all future centuries, will use all his malicious cunning to try to destroy this Convent, my foundation and property. Toward this end he will avail himself of persons of authority and dignity, and often under the pretext of improving the situation and bringing greater peace.

"Oh! The ignorance of the learned and the folly of mortals who do not recognize the secret designs of God in His works! Remember what the Royal Prophet sang: 'How marvelous are the works of the Lord!' Be convinced of this truth. Teach and impress upon your daughters living now and those to come that they should love their divine vocation. Let them know the glorious place that God and I are saving for those who belong to Us, Our heirs. God, the absolute Master of all that exists, of His own free will chooses where and how He will accomplish His secret designs, and no creature can thwart Him without incurring divine malediction. Throughout the centuries, I will live here in the person of some of my daughters. Here, amid the tumult of the ungrateful world, God will have some contemplative spouses worthy of His Majesty. Those souls, who will face obscurity, silence, humiliation, and scorn even from within the bosom of their community, will be strong forces to placate Divine Justice and earn great benefits for the Church, their Country, and their fellowman. Without them, Quito would not continue to exist."

For this reason, Our Lady of Good Success instructed Mother Mariana, it was the wish of Her Most Holy Son that a statue be made of her, just as she now appeared, and that it should be placed on the Abbess' chair so that she might govern her Convent until the end of time. In her right hand would be the crosier, and in her left arm, her Divine Child.

Our Lord desired that this statue be made for two reasons, she told Mother Mariana: "First, so that men in the future might realize how powerful I am in placating divine justice and obtaining mercy and pardon for every sinner who comes to me with a contrite heart. For I am the Mother of Mercy and in me there is only goodness and love."

"And second," she continued, "so that throughout time my daughters will see that I am giving to them My most Holy Son and their God as a Model of religious perfection. They should come to me, for I will lead them to Him. When the tribulations of spirit and sufferings of body oppress them and they seem to be drowning in this bottomless sea, let them gaze at my holy image and I will be like the star for the shipwrecked. I will always be there, ready to listen to their cries and soothe their pain. Tell them that they should always run to their Mother with confidence and love, for it is my desire to live with them and in them. Amid all their sufferings I will preserve their Convent until the end of time.

"Tell them that they should imitate my humility, my obedience, my spirit of sacrifice, and my absolute dependence on the Divine Will. These are the wings by which my daughters throughout the ages who venerate the mystery of my Immaculate Conception [8] will soar with mysterious agility to the highest summits of sanctity in the quiet retirement of their cloisters under the pure gaze of God."

---

[8] Even before the dogma of the Immaculate Conception was proclaimed by Blessed Pope Pius IX, it was always celebrated in the Franciscan Order. One of the many prophecies that Our Lady of Good Success revealed to Mother Mariana was that this teaching would be proclaimed a dogma of the Church in the 19th century, along with the dogma of Papal Infallibility. In fact, with the Bull *Ineffabilis*, Pope Pius IX solemnly proclaimed the dogma of the Immaculate Conception in 1854. The dogma of Papal Infallibility was proclaimed by the same Pontiff on July 18, 1870 during the First Vatican Council. For this prophecy, see *Our Lady of Good Success – Prophecies for our Times*, p. 65.

"A Day Will Come..."

Our Lady then spoke of the recent separation of the Convent from the governance of the Franciscans, a separation that has continued to our days, but which is destined to finally end in the future days of a happy restoration.

"The separation of my Friars Minor that has taken place is by divine permission," she said. "Woe to those who openly strive to obscure the light [of St. Francis] from this, my Convent. But after some centuries they will return to govern my beloved flock, which will always lament their absence and feel their loss. Neither you nor your present-day sisters and daughters will see this happiness that is yet to dawn for this blessed Convent. However, make sacrifices and implore God to hasten this day that will come on earth, for today marks the beginning of a dark night.

"But golden times will come for this, my Convent. Then a prelate, my most beloved son, blessed and prized before God, will understand by divine light the necessity for the daughters of my Immaculate Conception to subject themselves in exact obedience to the Friars Minor for their sanctification and perfection .... The day will come when the corruption of customs in the world will have seemed to have reached an apex and when my agonizing Community will find itself overcome by bitterness and sorrow. Then the Friars Minor will uplift their downcast spirits, attract true and saintly vocations, and form religious worthy of the name."

Before these happy times, Our Lady told Mother Mariana, God Himself and the Seraphic St. Francis would chastise the Order and separate the wheat from the chaff, leaving only the true wheat and the most perfect fruit. Happy, blessed, and beloved of God would be the sons and daughters of that time.

A First Measurement and Release from Prison

Then Our Lady permitted Mother Mariana to measure her height for the statue. So that it might be exactly as she appeared, the Virgin Mother instructed the religious to take off the cord Mother Mariana wore around her waist. She held one end of the cord to Our Lady's feet. The Blessed Virgin took the other end and brought it to her forehead.

"Here, my daughter," Our Lady instructed her, "you have the measurement of the height of your Heavenly Mother [The cord stretched to the length of 5 feet 9 inches]. Send them to my servant Francisco del Castillo and describe to him my features and posture. He will do the exterior work on my image, for he has a good conscience and scrupulously observes the Commandments of God and of the Church. Only he is worthy of this grace. You, on your part must aid him with your prayers and humble sufferings."

That very day, exactly as Our Lady had foretold, Mother Mariana and the Founding Mothers were released from the prison and restored to the positions of honor and dignity in the Convent that their virtue merited.

But, for several reasons, Mother Mariana hesitated to relate to the Bishop the order Our Lady had given her. First, she feared that she would not be believed, and the Bishop might see this as another disturbing incident and decide to close her beloved Convent.

Second, an underlying current of rebellion still existed in the Convent, fostered in particular by the leader of the nonobservant sisters. Mother Mariana, who was given to see the state of this unfortunate creature's soul, realized that in her state of fury and impenitence, she would be condemned to Hell upon her death, which was imminent. To save the soul of this revolted sister, Mother Mariana agreed to suffer five years in Hell suffering the punishments that the rebellious sister would have endured for all eternity.[9] During those five years, which seemed

---

[9] Ibid., pp. 41-3.

more like centuries, Mother Mariana suffered without relief or divine consolation the physical and moral torments of hell. Since she had taken on herself the guilt of all the sins of her sister, suffering as if they were her own, these sins tormented her with their weight and their memory. She entertained not the least hope for relief or pardon, and felt herself far outside the favor of God and Mary Most Holy. During these hard years, all the visions and favors she had received in her life of religious, including the apparitions of Our Lady of Good Success, seemed mockeries. Only a cold despair and the idea that she was condemned remained to her. Those who study mystical theology understand the ways by which Our Lord purifies and refines those souls He wants to raise to high degrees of sublime perfection.

Finally, in the year 1610, the five years of intense suffering ended. Mother Mariana, radiant now of both soul and body, assisted at the deathbed of the converted sister. This former leader of the internal rebellion died peacefully in the arms of Mother Mariana, whom she now recognized as her benefactress and loved as intensely as she had hated before.

Our Lady Dispels Mother Mariana's Doubts

On January 20, 1610, Our Lady appeared again to Mother Mariana as she prayed in the lower choir at midnight to warn her that she should delay no longer in asking the Bishop that this statue be made. Our Lady explained to her that this image was destined to do a great good for the Convent and the whole world in the centuries to come. Through this devotion Our Lord would grant great miracles, spiritual as well as temporal, first to her community, and second, to the devout faithful, above all those at the end of the 18th and 20th centuries,[10] for the chosen ones of His Heart would live in those times, times dur-

---

[10] The end of the 18th century saw the French Revolution, with its disastrous consequences in the temporal sphere. The end of the 20th century saw the Ecumenical Council Vatican II and its consequences in the Church.

ing which Hell would be unleashed and many souls would be lost.[11]

The penitent religious begged pardon from Our Lady. She considered herself incapable of describing her queenly features and dazzling beauty to the sculptor, the religious said. Further, she still harbored fears that the Bishop would not believe her. She begged the Queen of Heaven, who knows all the events of the future, to show her the way to obey and please her, for this was Mother Mariana's only ambition on this earth.

To dispel these doubts and hasten her obedience, Our Lady sent to Mother Mariana her three celestial ambassadors, the Archangels St. Michael, St. Gabriel, and St. Raphael, accompanied by innumerable armies of Angels.

Approaching the religious, St. Gabriel sent forth a luminous ray that penetrated the mind of this fortunate religious and dissipated her doubts, just as the sun bursts forth in the dark early morning and its bright rays announce the beginning of a new day.

St. Michael thrust a second luminous ray into the heart of Mother Mariana, which penetrated its deepest fibers, inflaming it with a supernatural fire. She felt herself capable of undertaking the greatest deeds for the love of God and of her Heavenly Mother. At the same time, she realized the nothingness of her own being, as well as the infinite love of her God, Who had predestined her for the singular favor of familiar conversation with His Divine Majesty and Mary Most Holy.

Finally, St. Raphael approached her and said, "Our Lord has charged you to command that a statue of His Most Holy Mother be sculpted in conformance with her directives, and this statue will be venerated, especially in future centuries. I was sent to cure your blindness of mind so that you will believe the truth of these apparitions that you have rashly doubted until

---

[11] Our Lady described how the Sacraments would be profaned and forgotten, and the institutions of Church and State would be infiltrated by Freemasonry. *Our Lady of Good Success – Prophecies for our Times*, pp. 44-6.

now. From this day forward you will see their veracity more clearly and be relieved of these doubts, so abhorrent to God."

And the Archangel let fly a transparent ray into her mind and heart that pervaded her whole being. She saw then with great clarity her whole life and all the graces and favors throughout its course that she had received from the goodness of God and His Most Holy Mother. She also understood the veracity of all the apparitions and how her soul had needed all the sufferings through which she had passed, for these sufferings are requisite for every soul that Our Lord calls to walk on an extraordinary pathway.

The Archangels withdrew, and Mother Mariana prepared herself to receive again the Queen of Heaven, whose presence the celestial ambassadors had announced.

The Importance of Religious Vocations

Prostrate on the ground, her arms stretched out in the form of a cross, Mother Mariana thanked Our Lord for having bestowed upon her such divine favors and offered to God all that He might ask of her. With her heart inflamed with love and illuminated with the divine rays of supernatural understanding, she received the visit from the Celestial Queen who carried the Infant Jesus in her arms.

On the arm that carried the crosier perched some sickly doves that were struggling to leave the arm of their Mother. But the Divine Child tried to detain and divert them, caressing them and offering them small pieces of bread. Mary Most Holy spoke to them with maternal sweetness, but they paid no attention to her words. Against their will they remained on her arm and became increasingly weak. Finally, after exhausting every means to win them with charity and love, the Divine Child took them and thrust them down into the tempestuous sea of the world. Lacking strength to survive, they began to sink into the profound abyss. They cried out in despair as they realized too late that they had lost a good that had been theirs to enjoy forever in exchange for a little effort, suffering, and sacrifice.

Our Lady explained this vision to her: "You cannot comprehend how much We love sinners! Created as they were for heaven, a great multitude nonetheless will be lost because they refuse to suffer and do but a little violence to themselves.

"You saw those sickly doves? Now understand, my daughter, that they are the religious unfaithful to their vocation who, throughout the course of the centuries, will try to flee our protective embrace. You saw with what fondness and tenderness my Most Holy Son and I treated them? We shall always help them in this way, drawing them to us and nourishing them with the Eucharistic Host. But, alas, those ungrateful ones will turn their backs to us. Finally, exhausting the mercy and patience of my Most Holy Son, they will be abandoned and fall into the turbulent ocean of the world, where, oppressed by sufferings and sorrows and tormented by their uneasy consciences, many of them will lose their souls.

"Observe them well, so that you might know all those here in this Convent."

Then Mother Mariana de Jesus looked, and saw all of the unfaithful religious who would live in her beloved Convent from the first to the last until the end of time. Her first instinct was to throw herself prostrate before Divine Justice and plead their cause, but the Queen of Heaven continued to speak:

"Daughter, neither I nor you can avert this great misfortune insomuch as God Himself respects the free will of His creatures. They will not lack lights, graces, inspirations, and the charitable counsel and warnings of their Superiors, nor the example of many good religious who will pray for them and sweetly admonish them. They, however, will remain deaf. Because of their inveterate lukewarmness, God justly abandons such souls, who, by their own volition, make themselves unworthy of the sublime grace of the religious vocation and thus receive, as you see, their just chastisement.

"But moderate your sorrow, beloved daughter, by considering this enormous number of faithful souls who here in my beloved Convent will live and die in self-abnegation and isolation, practicing the solid virtues in heroism and hidden sanctity.

Through them in the future centuries, as well as through you in these times, Divine Justice will be stayed."

As she saw all her faithful daughters throughout time, Mother Mariana was given to understand that these religious, who belong wholly to God, glorify Him more by their total sacrifice of self than almost all other acts of devotion. It is the reign of God in man and the death of self-love. Consequently, it is a very great grace when Our Lord calls souls to the interior life to live with Him and be wholly occupied with Him.

The Mission of the Statue of Our Lady of Good Success

Our Lady then told Mother Mariana of the great crisis that would continue through the last half of the 20th century. [12] Because of the severity of these times that would come, Our Lady said, she desired this statue to be made so that she might be, under this invocation, "the consolation and preservation of my Convent and of those faithful souls of that epoch during which there will be a great devotion to me. This devotion will be the lightning rod placed between Divine Justice and the prevaricating world to hold back God's Hand from unleashing the formidable punishment that this guilty earth deserves."

"This very day," she told Mother Mariana, "you should go to the Bishop and tell him that I have asked and commanded you to have my image sculpted, to be placed at the head of my community so that, under this title, I might take possession of that which belongs to me. And, as proof of what you say, tell him that he will die in two years and two months, and that he should even now begin to prepare himself for the day of eternity, for his death will be a sudden and violent one.

"He should consecrate my statue with Holy Oil and give to it the name of Mary of Good Success of the Purification, or Candlemas. On this solemn occasion, he himself should place the keys of the cloister, together with the crosier, in the right hand of my statue, as proof that the government of my Son's

---

[12] Ibid., pp. 44-9.

spouses here has been entrusted to me, so that they might entrust all their concerns to my maternal and loving protection.

"Then tell the governing Bishop, whose passions and indiscretions are sowing dissension and rancor among the Clergy and the people, that every Prelate, without exception, should be the father of all his people in imitation of the Divine Pastor Jesus Christ, Who said, 'Learn of Me, for I am meek and humble of Heart.' He should endeavor to save all those entrusted to Him ....

"Realize well that mortal life is the time given to creatures [to perfect themselves]. But the hour of God will come, and then He will take into the most strict and severe account every action of His creatures and all of its consequences. Then will He judge and sentence each one with perfect equity. I permitted you to see what will happen to your sisters who worked for the separation of the Friars Minor after they had passed to eternity. How many of these sisters will suffer [in Purgatory] until the Franciscans return, and others until the Day of Judgment! In all times let religious souls tremble should they fall away from the perfect observance of their Rules!"

That evening Mother Mariana called together the Founding Mothers to speak with them and ask their advice. They counseled her to call the Bishop and tell him everything, just as she had done with them. They immediately began to pray that all would go forward quickly so that they might soon possess the treasure of this sacred statue, which would be bequeathed to all their successors and would be the assurance of the stability of the Community that had cost them all so many sacrifices, tears, and suffering. Further, they were greatly consoled to know that some day the Friars Minor would return to direct and govern the Convent.

* * *

Chapter III

AFTER A LONG DELAY, THE WORK BEGINS

Nonetheless, Mother Mariana mysteriously hesitated. Twelve days later on February 2, 1610, Our Lady of Good Success appeared again, this time angry with her daughter. By delaying in carrying out this command, Our Lady told her, she was thwarting the Divine Will and the many graces it would bring.

To understand this hesitation and delay of Mother Mariana, one need only consider that throughout time the devil works to stop projects that, by a preternatural sense, he foresees will do a great good for souls. In this case, the evil spirit was doing all he could to impede the making of this statue that would offer great benefit during these troubled times in the Convent and Colony, as well as in the centuries to come. For the spirit of darkness perceived that this statue would act as a serious obstacle to the realization of his plans. He also sensed the providential role devotion to this statue would play in his defeat by the Queen of Heaven in centuries to come.

Our Lady confirmed to Mother Mariana the roles the statue and Convent would play in the future: "With the making of my statue I will favor not only you and my Convent, but also the people of this city, and many more in other nations throughout the centuries. This Convent will be a fortress and bring salvation to many souls, for it will draw many souls from the abyss of sin in which they find themselves. God will be glorified in them. How many conversions it will bring about!"

Mother Mariana humbled herself before her Queen, and like a child before her mother, explained her fears and pleaded for a special grace that would make her task less difficult. In particular, she said, she harbored a personal fear that the native people, who were still inclined to idolatry, might regard her, the Spanish Mother, with too great honor should they learn of her role in all this. Therefore, she asked the grace that her own name would be hidden so that Mary Most Holy alone might be glorified.

A Grace is Granted and the Doubts Dispelled

Pleased with the humility of her daughter, the Queen of Heaven pardoned her fault against obedience. She also promised that she would prepare the Bishop to respond favorably, for the time that remained to him on this earth was short, and he had been chosen to consecrate her statue with holy oil.

"Tell him," she instructed Mother Mariana, "that at his final agony, we – you and I – will be there at his side to help him in his final anguish. If he asks you how you will come to find yourself there, tell him that nothing is impossible for God and His Most Holy Mother, for They are the absolute masters of all their creatures."

In fact, that very night, Our Lady was preparing the Bishop to receive Mother Mariana's request by sending him a prophetic dream, which included a warning of his approaching death.

As for her plea that her name be hidden, Our Lady promised to grant her request: "Tell the Bishop that it is my will and that of my Most Holy Son that your name be hidden at all costs, both inside as well as outside the cloister, for it is not our desire that anyone now should know the details of how this statue came to be made. For this knowledge will become known to the general public in the 20th century." [13]

As for Mother Mariana de Jesus Torres' fears that she could never adequately describe Our Lady's beauty, the Queen of Heaven assured her, "Do not worry about the features of my statue, for I will appear as I desire in order to fulfill the final ends for which this statue is destined." For, she told her, "the work would be sculpted not by the hands of mortal men, but by

---

[13] For more on this prophecy, in which Our Lady warned of the corruption of customs, unbridled luxury, an impious press and secular education system, see *Our Lady of Good Success – Prophecies for Our Times*, p. 49.

the Seraphic Father St. Francis and by the supernatural action of the three Archangels."

Again the Cord Stretches Miraculously

Then, once again, the Virgin Most Pure granted Mother Mariana the great favor of measuring her height. Again, Mother Mariana took off the corded belt of her habit and placed one end at the feet of her majestic Queen. As the religious raised her eyes to contemplate the forehead of her Mother, she saw that the Divine Child had taken the other end of the cord and had touched it to the top of the forehead of His Holy Mother. He was gazing with love at this creature, whom He had adorned with every grace, gift and virtue.

Extending His small, gracious hand, He handed the cord to Mother Mariana. This act, He told her, was symbolic of how religious should be measured throughout time: "And do you know how I desire that they be measured? I shall measure their humility, their silence, their charity, their patience, their love for Me and My Most Holy Mother, whom they should mirror in all things. And as with all the faithful, and even more with religious, I desire that they should imbue every act of their lives with My Spirit. Know that My Spirit is that of patience, meekness, abnegation, and total abandonment to the Divine Will. Let them serve Me with diligence and disinterest, and let them offer even their eternal happiness to the loving will of My Divine Heart.

"So that I might take My delight among religious souls, My dearly beloved spouses, I remain hidden under the accidents of bread in the Sacrament of the Eucharist, exposing Myself to the irreverence and profanation of My enemies. If these latter often torment Me, I find My satisfaction in the loving redress of those favored souls who live with Me under the same roof; thus do I receive their caresses and live in them through every type of suffering. What does it matter to them that they live here on earth in complete obscurity when, in Heaven, their names will resound among the number of the blessed?

"During these first centuries, I desire that your name remain hidden, just as the names of My [other] heroic spouses throughout time will be hidden, those who will live in this Convent to comfort Me and to hold back the arm of Divine Justice, so ready to release itself upon this ungrateful land."

The heart of this humble religious was flooded with happiness and love of God. Returning to herself, she found herself a second time holding a cord that had miraculously stretched. Standing before her were the Founding Mothers, who were asking her to begin the Little Office of the Blessed Virgin, which it was custom for all the novices to recite at 4 a.m. every morning. All the Spanish Mothers would assist at this devotion that brought so many blessings to the Convent.

Sensing that something unusual had happened, the Founding Mothers asked God and their Most Holy Mother that they might be worthy to know and assist in the fulfillment of the Divine Will. Mother Mariana was silent, but later that morning at the Convent Mass, while the Eucharistic God rested in their hearts during their thanksgiving after Communion, they were all given to understand what had taken place that morning. When the occasion arose that day to speak again with their Mother Superior, they pleaded that she might speak to the Bishop and reveal the whole apparition, from beginning to end.

Taking Counsel With her Spiritual Director

Before taking this step, Mother Mariana went to her spiritual director, Friar Juan de la Madre de Dios Mendoza, a noble Spanish religious of outstanding virtue. This saintly Franciscan, who wrote a biography of this humble and hidden servant of God, died in the odor of sanctity in 1636, one year after Mother Mariana's death. From his eyewitness testimony, we have the account of the many favors she received from Heaven, as well as her continuous sufferings and penances, which would seem incredible to persons little versed in the supernatural life.

She confided all that had taken place to this wise director of souls, who instructed her that the whole community should pray and make special penances that day so that he might know the will of God in this important matter. Prolonging his prayers late into the night, the priest was granted a vision of Our Lady of Good Success, exactly as she had appeared to Mother Mariana with the Divine Infant in her left arm. The Seat of Wisdom confirmed to him her desire that this holy statue be made, revealing to him the ends for which God intended it until the last day of the world and the many benefits and graces that souls would receive through this devotion.

The next day, he met again with Mother Mariana de Jesus Torres. "The Most Holy Trinity confirmed the desire of my Queen," he said. "And I was assured that God will bless all those who, by their support and help, contribute in the making of this holy statue, as well as all those who help to spread this devotion throughout the centuries, making known its origin and these apparitions in the 20th century. This will be a time of great corruption of customs, and this devotion will be a great safeguard both inside and outside the Convent. Let us weep, pray, and do penance so that this time will not be of long duration. Mother, God desires this of us; it is He Who asks this of us."

Having said those words, he ordered her to call upon the Bishop immediately, to tell him everything openly and simply. After giving her his blessing, this holy Priest returned to his monastery.

The Bishop's Response

Mother Mariana forthwith sent the Bishop a message expressing her urgent need to speak with him, if possible, even that day. Bishop Salvador de Ribera had woken fatigued and disturbed by the disquieting dream of his death. However, he was well aware that this holy Mother Superior had suffered much at the hands of the rebellious sisters in her Convent, and fearing that some new rebellion was underfoot, he agreed to meet with her that very day. When he arrived, she asked to speak with him in the confessional. There she proceeded to reveal all that occurred in the apparition of February 2.

The Bishop listened with great attention and astonishment. Finally he spoke: "Mother, why did Your Reverence not call me sooner? For it is God Who so disposes this, and we should not remain deaf to His voice or His request. He is free to ask of His creatures whatsoever pleases Him."

From the depths of her heart, Mother Mariana breathed a great sign of relief upon hearing these words.

Then the Prelate added: "Mother, it comes as a hard realization to know that I shall die so soon. What are two years? If it were possible for you to ask Our Lord to prolong my life, how happy I would be! I ask Your Reverence to obtain this grace for her Prelate. In the meantime, I will begin to take the necessary measures so that the request of our Heavenly Queen might be carried out. I ask your special prayers for me. I will join you and your whole community in making a novena to the Holy Ghost. At the end of the nine days, I will return to speak with Your Reverence about how to proceed with the making of the statue."

The First Steps

During the nine days of the novena, the Bishop nourished not the least hope that his request for a longer life might be granted, and he began to prepare himself for his journey into eternity. He had been planning to return to Spain after three more years so that he might rest from the fatigues and trials of governing the unruly and fractious Colony. Now he recognized his many imprudent actions in governing the Diocese and resolved to amend his life.

Bishop Ribera was very young when he entered the Dominican Order and had become celebrated early as a skilled preacher with a vast knowledge of theology. Because of his great learning and skills, he had come to occupy offices of authority not only within but also outside his Order. None of this, however, would be of any value to him at his Judgment, for honors alone without the practices of virtue account for nothing in the eyes of the God of Sanctity and Justice.

For Bishop Salvador de Ribera had been strongly influenced by pride in the nobility of his family. He had adopted the view that the natives of Quito were all lazy and fickle *mestizos*. With them, as with the Colony's clerics and friars, he exerted a stern and hard zeal, like steel. At the same time, he favored members of his own family and catered to those in high positions. Consequently, he did not enjoy great popularity among the people, something that only further vexed his vanity. He suffered all the more in that his predecessor, Bishop Luis López de Solis, had been a holy Prelate beloved by all. Seeking honors neither for himself nor his family, indefatigable in his labors for the souls under his care, he had been a true man of God.

At the end of the nine days, Bishop Ribera returned to speak to Mother Mariana. He asked her many questions to see if she would contradict herself on any point and to determine the spirit that animated her. Each response of this humble religious constituted for him a torrent of light through which he discerned the Spirit of God. The Prelate realized the great intelligence and gifts that Our Lord had conceded to this holy soul, and he was moved to command her to tell him all the graces and favors with which Our Lord had favored her throughout her life. Docile and obedient, Mother Mariana made a full account, including the favors she had received during her four unjust imprisonments, as well as the torments she had endured during the five years she had spent in Hell to save the soul of the leader of the rebellious sisters.

Struck with deep shame that he had permitted the persecution of such a saintly creature, the Bishop exclaimed, "Mother, I realize that Your Reverence unjustly suffered what should be reserved only for a great sinner. I confess that I did not support you as I should have."

Her reply made the Bishop realize even better the grandeur of this soul: "Your Excellency, such sufferings and unjust humiliations are jewels of priceless value that God puts in our hands so that we might purchase Heaven. Why, then, should we refuse them? Never will I complain of my past sufferings."

He then turned to the matter of the statue, and gave orders that all should be carried out as soon as possible. "I myself will have the silver keys made at my own expense," he said. "And upon these keys I shall order a cross to be placed, since without the cross, the gates of Heaven will not open. But I still remain in anguish that my end is already so near."

Mother Mariana responded: "To live in this arid desert of our earthly existence is not to live, Your Excellency. Leave this mortal life and soar to the regions of eternity! Fortitude! Courage! Put your soul in order before God and rest tranquilly in the sleep of the just, awaiting the final resurrection. We will not forget you in our prayers. I will await you in Heaven, for even though I shall die long after Your Excellency, I will ascend before you to Heaven."

The Bishop sighed upon hearing this. Then, after giving her his blessing and asking for her prayers and those of her sisters, he left.

The Sculptor is Called

That very day, the holy Abbess sent for Francisco del Castillo, a man of noble lineage from Valladolid and a sculptor of some fame in the Colony. He and his wife, Dona Maria Javiera, were virtuous and upright souls who had a deep love for the Queen of Angels and fasted in her honor every Saturday in accordance with a vow they had made when they were married.

"*Señor*," she greeted him, "as I realize that you are above all, a good Catholic, and, in addition to this, a skilled sculptor, I wish to confide to you a very special work that will require great effort on your part."

She explained that he would sculpt a statue of the Most Holy Virgin under the invocation of Good Success. It would not be like the one venerated in Spain, but one made especially for the Colony. "It should not be an ordinary statue. It should have life," she said. "I will give you its measurements, for the statue will have the exact height of Our Heavenly Queen."

As the Mother Abbess spoke, the artisan felt an ineffable expansion of soul and intense desire to increase his knowledge, love, and service to God and His Holy Mother. He realized that there was something sublime and supernatural in this work, and he thanked Mother Mariana for the great favor of having chosen him to make it. It was determined that he would complete his other commissions and then make a trip outside the Colony to find an extremely hard wood for this statue that was destined to last until the end of time. In early Fall, he would begin the work. To facilitate his work and permit him frequent consultations with Mother Mariana about how the statue should appear, the Bishop granted him a special permission to work in the upper choir [which was cloistered and normally reserved only for the sisters] since this was the place that Our Lady desired to be placed to govern her Convent.

The Work Begins

After imploring God for enlightenment and grace to make a statue worthy of His Blessed Mother, the sculptor confessed and received Communion with his wife in the Convent church on September 15, 1610. Then he began the work. For the next weeks as the statue began to take shape under his chisel, he was like a man transformed, joyous, the love of God and His Holy Mother enveloping his being, and often tears of unction streaming from his eyes.

In fact, Our Lady did not delay in showing her gratitude to the good sculptor for his participation in the celestial work. His first child, Maria, entered the Convent of the Immaculate Conception of Quito with the name of Maria of the Angels shortly after the holy statue was sculpted and consecrated with Holy Oils. Francisco, the second, became a Franciscan and was sent to Spain, where he became renowned as a preacher and man of great virtue. The last, Manuel, entered into the bonds of holy matrimony with a virtuous girl from the Colony, and from them came the del Castillo family in Quito. During this time, a spirit of admiration and joy reigned in the Convent. The other sisters sensed the supernatural ambience that surrounded the work even though they did not know about the apparitions of Our Lady. The Mother Abbess only told the Community that it was the will of God and His Most Holy Mother that this beautiful statue be made under the invocation of Good Success. She told them that the statue would be placed in the Abbess' chair, and that the keys to the cloister and crosier would be placed in her right hand so that she might rule and govern the Community *in aeternum*. The statue would carry the Divine Child on her left arm so that Our Lady might placate the divine ire and throughout time give good successes to all who, with faith and love, had recourse to her. And she exhorted them to pray much that the work should proceed according to the will and pleasure of God.

*   *   *

Chapter IV

THE MARQUESA[14] AND THE BISHOP

In great works, Our Lord disposes that certain generous souls will cooperate with grace and offer the material means to carry out His plans. In this work, God so disposed that a holy widow, the Marquesa Maria de Yolanda, would befriend the Convent of the Immaculate Conception. The Marquesa, whose family was related to the King of Spain, had various properties in Spain as well as rural houses in the Colony and enjoyed many privileges. However, she chose to live in the city of Quito rather than on one of her country properties because of her devotion to the sisters of the Convent of the Immaculate Conception. In particular, she had a great love for Mother Mariana, whom she considered a saint and often consulted on many matters.

It was natural that the Mother Abbess should turn to this generous soul to ask her help in financing the crosier for the statue. For while the Bishop had offered to donate the keys for the statue, and the chapter would present the crown, the Conceptionist community would be responsible for the crosier. At the same time, Mother Mariana determined to grant the Marquesa the great favor of standing as godmother to the statue on the day it would be consecrated with Holy Oils and solemnly installed in the Abbess' Chair.

In September 1610, when the sculpture had reached the exact height of Mother Mariana's cord, she chose to invite the noble lady to assist in the execution of the project. Thus, she sent a message to the Marquesa, who, excitable by nature, rushed to the Convent to see what aid she might offer the sisters whom she admired so greatly.

---

[14] In Spain a *marqués* (or marquis in English) is a nobleman next in rank above a count. His wife or widow is titled *marquesa* in Spanish, the form that will be used in this book, or marchioness in English.

Mother Mariana described the great project that the Convent was undertaking and asked her assistance in the making of the crosier.

"Mother," responded the Marquesa, "how sorely offended I would have been if Your Reverence had not come to me first. I thank you for your attention and fondness, and I assure you that I will not even consider that anyone else should contribute toward the making of this crosier for the statue of my celestial Mother and Lady. I will furnish all the material and the cost of labor. I have sufficient means for this. Yet, even if I did not, I would sell my belongings in order to have this crosier made."

With the magnanimity proper to grand souls, she insisted that she would cover all the expenses for sculpting the image, which, she further offered, could be made in her house. Mother Mariana thanked her for this gesture, but explained that Francisco del Castillo had already commenced the work and had refused any payment except for the prayers of the community and their successors.

"The work is going ahead," Mother Mariana assured her. "Already the statue possesses the height that the Queen of Heaven requested."

The heart of the Marquesa began to pound in her chest as she sensed something most sublime in this news. "Mother, what is this that I hear?" she exclaimed. "I will not return to my home without first knowing the height of this statue. I can and should participate in the mercies of Mary Most Holy, since I call myself Maria de Yolanda, child and slave of the Queen of Heaven.

"I cannot move my left arm, as a consequence of a severe break I suffered three days ago in these wretched streets of the city. For this reason, I must return home soon to meet with the doctor. But first, I beg Your Reverence to reveal to me this measurement. With this favor I will already be well paid for the little that I am going to do for you."

The First Miracle of Our Lady of Good Success

Mother Mariana returned with one of the two miraculous cords, which she placed in the hands of the Marquesa, who cried out with joy and pressed it against her heart with both hands. She did not even realize that she had moved her injured arm, such was her transport of joy, although Mother Mariana saw this favor from Our Lady of Good Success and said nothing.

A moment later, she said, "Thank you, Mother, for this great favor. I return this cord with the greatest gratitude."

The Abbess received the cord and responded, "The Holy Virgin will requite your faith and devotion, good lady," and then bade her farewell to return to her duties..

When the Marquesa arrived at her house, the maids marveled at the transformation. "What has happened to our mistress, who left with a broken arm and returned cured?' they asked. "To which saint did she recommend herself?"

A few moments later, the doctor arrived for a routine examination. He immediately noticed the movement in her arm and questioned the Marquesa about what had happened. Only then did she realize the great favor Our Lady had granted her. She explained to the doctor what had happened.

"*Señora*, this was certainly a miracle!" he said, but without surprise, for he knew the virtues and merits of the Mother Abbess. "For, humanly speaking, no one could have cured that arm. The break was quite severe and needed to be set for at least three long, pain-filled months."

Later that day, the Marquesa returned to the Convent to relate the miracle to Mother Mariana. The next day she wrote to her relatives in Spain, giving a precise description of the crosier she wanted made by the best goldsmiths they could find and to be completed as quickly as possible, without regard to cost.

The Story of the Unjustly Condemned Shoemaker

May the reader permit a brief interruption in the narration of the making of the statue to hear an incident that illustrates the great valor of the Marquesa, and also how quickly Our Lady of Good Success began to mediate on behalf of the people of Quito.

A simple shoemaker, an honorable Christian who lived in the environs of San Bras, was delivering orders to some homes one day when a man running at breakneck speed crossed his path. Since the shoemaker had not been able to see his face, he ran after the fleeing man to see if he could recognize him. Doing this, the shoemaker was unaware he was following a criminal and that he himself might fall suspect to the police who were not far behind. Unfortunately, however, this happened. The police apprehended the shoemaker, whom they assumed to be the fleeing criminal who had committed a brutal murder, cutting his victim into various pieces that had been found in diverse places in the city.

The poor shoemaker protested his innocence, but was not believed. He was immediately taken before the magistrate and sentenced to death. His Augustinian confessor, who was called to attend him before his execution, questioned the distraught man. Convinced of his innocence, the priest tried to intervene with the authorities, but to no avail. He could only confess and attempt to encourage the man, reminding him of the example of Our Lord Jesus Christ, who died innocent for man's sake. But the shoemaker, in despair at leaving his wife and children destitute, could not be comforted.

When she heard the news, his poor wife, crazed in grief, began to go from house to house, begging assistance from any who would listen to save the life of her innocent husband. Finally she reached the house of the Marquesa. She told her everything and implored her protection on behalf of her husband. The Marquesa, who had many influential friends, managed to gain a stay of execution for the man. He remained in prison, however, humiliated and fearful that each day might be his last.

The Impasse is Resolved

During this interim, the Marquesa spoke with Mother Mariana, asking her to beg Our Lady that justice might be done: If the man were guilty, then he should pay for his crime with his life. But if he were innocent, let some proof be given so that he might return to his family. Moved with compassion, Mother Mariana promised to ask Our Lady that she give good success to this poor man.

That very night, an artisan in the city fell victim to a severe attack of fever and entered into his last agony. He asked to receive Confession. Providence permitted that the same Augustinian priest who had confessed the innocent shoemaker should now arrive at the bedside of the real criminal. The dying artisan confessed the horrendous crime, committed in the passion of revenge. When he learned that an innocent man would die for his crime, he had become desolate, since he lacked the courage to confess his crime publicly. That very morning, he had gone to the Church of the Immaculate Conception to hear Mass and implore God's pardon for his action. He had asked that he might become sick and die, so that he could confess and die with his conscience at peace. His request had been granted, and now he asked the confessor to tell the authorities that he was the true culprit so that the innocent man might be set free.

The next day the shoemaker was released from prison. Even before returning to his home to embrace his wife, he went to the house of the Marquesa. On his knees, he thanked her for having delivered him from death. The Marquesa assured the man that it was not she that he should thank, but the holy sisters in her beloved Convent of the Immaculate Conception whose prayers had been heard by Our Lady of Good Success.

Having learned of the poverty of the family whose rent was now past due on the humble quarters they occupied, the good Marquesa invited him to live in one of her houses. She would not demand any rent, but only ask that he and his wife frequent the Sacraments and live honorably. He accepted this offer with gratitude, and thus this man, his wife, and his children served the noble Marquesa faithfully until her death. Moreover, in her will she did not forget them and left means for their support.

The Dream of Bishop Ribera

On December 15, while the statue was being made, Bishop Salvador de Ribera had a terrifying dream that acted as a further warning for him to amend his life and come to terms with himself and his actions. He saw himself overcome by a sudden and violent illness, which left him without life after several days of suffering. In his last agony, he saw Mother Mariana de Jesus Torres at his bedside. She raised her clear blue eyes to Heaven and begged mercy and pity for her Prelate, who was being accused of the many serious faults he had committed in his harsh and self-serving government of the Diocese. He understood, then, how terrible would be the judgment of God and he searched for something that might placate the Divine Justice, but could find nothing.

At the height of his anguish, the Blessed Virgin approached, carrying in her hands a set of silver keys. Kneeling before the dreaded judgment seat of God, she said: "This son of mine delivered to me the keys of the cloisters of the Convent of My Immaculate Conception. Now, let these keys close the terrible Tribunal of Justice and open that of infinite Mercy, for these keys represent the unceasing prayers of the daughters of My Immaculate Heart for this servant of mine." And, with that, a judgment of mercy commenced, after which he saw the long years destined to him for the purification of his soul in the expiatory fires of Purgatory before he might enter Heaven.

In his terror and grief, the Bishop awoke with a cry. Uncertain at first if he were still truly alive, he got up, dressed, and began to pray the Rosary, a devotion that he had learned in the Order of St. Dominic and that he had always loved and practiced.

Our Lord Reveals His Mercy for the Bishop of Quito to Mother Mariana

That same night of December 15 as Mother Mariana was praying before the Most Holy Sacrament, she saw the Tabernacle open and the whole corner of the sanctuary become illuminated with a celestial light. There she contemplated the Most Holy Trinity, present in the Sacred Host.

The Divine Word presented Himself at His age of perfection vested as a Bishop and Pastor of His beloved flock. He told her: "My favored spouse, how My Heart desires that Bishops and Pastors would be true fathers to all their children. But, behold My sorrow! For the empty delights of learning, nobility, and wealth blind the minds of Prelates and topple that grand edifice of pastoral charity that should be raised so high by the Pastors of the Church....

"Today you see Me vested as Pastor and Bishop so that I might manifest My love for My cherished flock. Especially do I manifest My love for this Colony, which suffers so greatly from the many imprudences of its present Bishop. You do well to plead for his salvation, for his guilt is great.

"He is, however, a religious of the Dominican Order, so beloved by My Most Holy Mother, and from which he learned that sweet devotion of the Marian Psalter [the Rosary]. And Divine Justice will never remain deaf to those who practice this devotion with diligence and zeal. The Bishop loves My Most Holy Mother. He honors her with the Rosary, and he will place in her almost omnipotent hands the keys to this cloister so beloved by her. Because of this, he will be judged with mercy on the day of his death, which will take place on March 24, 1612, a year after the statue of my Most Holy Mother will be placed in this choir.

"He will consecrate this statue with Holy Oil, making her Superior and Mother Abbess of this community so that she might reign here until the end of time. Here, then, in this sanctuary, all sinners and afflicted souls might always find pardon for their sins as well as consolation and answers for all their needs and tribulations. For this reason, My Most Holy Mother wishes to be known under that tender invocation of Good Success."

Even as He was speaking to her, Our Lord continued, the Bishop was receiving a dream and a great grace that would permit him to come to terms with himself before his death.

"Know that the prayers of religious souls penetrate the Heart of God," Our Lord told the Mother Abbess, "and they obtain what the world is powerless to attain .... Therefore, you and your religious should pray for Prelates, for the Church, and for this guilty Colony. Know that here I live and will always live with My beloved daughters, who will never be lacking to Me."

With these words, the vision ended. Mother Mariana de Jesus Torres returned to her senses and, her heart overflowing with love of God, continued to pray in the choir until her community arrived to recite the Little Office at 4 a.m., a devotion that brings a great blessing on the city of Quito.

*   *   *

Chapter V

The Angels Finish the
Statue of Our Lady of Good Success

On January 2, 1611, the Marquesa received the crosier from Spain, her gift to the Holy Statue to be offered on the day of its consecration. Along with it, she had also ordered a small, finely worked golden brooch in the form of a peahen, which carried in its beak a golden scroll adorned with precious stones. The scroll was engraved with the Marquesa's monogram and the date February 2, 1611.

One week later, she presented these gifts to Mother Mariana. In return, she said, she asked only for prayers from the religious who lived in those blessed cloisters. She also offered dowries for five girls – in honor of the five letters that compose the name Maria – so that they might enter the religious life.

After receiving these precious gifts in the turnbox of the Convent's visiting room, Mother Mariana surprised the Marquesa by inviting her to join her in the visiting room. Weeping with joy, she found all the Founding Mothers who embraced their noble benefactress. Her joy became near ecstasy when she learned that the statue was very near to being finished.

"Now, we have another favor to ask of you, my Lady," said Mother Mariana. "We ask that you would accept the office of being the godmother of the Holy Statue. Mary Most Holy, our Mother, has chosen you for this and requests your consent."

"Mother, what am I hearing?!" exclaimed the Marquesa, overwhelmed by the honor. She gave her assent with joy, "Now, I am certain of seeing Heaven, for it is in the hands of my Godchild, and she will open it for me... A thousand thanks, Mother, a thousand thanks."

The next day, January 10, the Bishop came to see the work. Finding it almost complete and very well made, he congratulated the artist. He then exhorted him to take the greatest care with the final step – the last coat of paint – so that the work might be worthy of the Mother of God.

When the Bishop left, the sculptor told the Mothers that he could proceed no further until he had acquired the best and finest of paints, which were not available in Quito. He assured the religious that he would make the greatest haste possible to acquire the materials. He would return six days later on the 16th to complete the work. Then, after receiving Holy Communion, he would undertake the final and most delicate step of painting the statue.

An Air of Expectation in the Convent

As the work progressed, the religious in the Royal Convent of the Immaculate Conception could think and speak of nothing but the statue. They would say to each other "How fortunate we are! The Queen of Heaven and Her Most Holy Son are going to live among us, and she will govern us. Now, more than ever do we have the obligation to be holy!" Then they would thank Our Lady for having given them such a model of holiness in their Abbess, who had suffered so many persecutions and trials, and lived among them then and now more like an angel than a human.

In these happy days, each sister strove to become more perfect, and made many acts of penance and public humiliations imploring God that the final work might be the best possible so that the statue of their Most Holy Mother might be venerated throughout the centuries.

The 15th of January finally arrived. The sculptor would arrive the next morning after Mass to complete the work. That night the sisters went to their Abbess and told her that they had determined to pray the Little Office the next morning with redoubled fervor and with the express request that Our Lady herself might complete her statue.

"You do well, my daughters" said Mother Mariana, for she had been forewarned interiorly during the community prayer that evening to prepare herself, for she would soon witness Our Lord's mercy toward the Convent and mankind in general. "Let us ask this with humble insistence and she will do as we request. Our supplications will please her Most Holy Son, Who will help us in this. For no one loves His Most Holy Mother as He does."

The Marvels that Mother Mariana Witnesses

At midnight, as Mother Mariana ended her customary exercise of the Stations of the Cross, she entered the upper choir to pray before the unfinished statue. Celestial lights illuminated the Church and upper choir, and she saw the Tabernacle open. In the Host, she saw the Father, the Son and the Holy Ghost. Then she saw the throne of the Divine Majesty as well as the throne of Our Lady, and she realized the infinite love of the Three Divine Persons for Mary Most Holy. The nine Angelic Choirs sang praises and rendered homage to her as their Queen and Lady.

At a gesture from the Holy Trinity, the Archangels Michael, Gabriel, and Raphael presented themselves before the throne of the Divine Majesty, as if to receive some sublime command. They bowed as a sign of profound reverence and acquiescence, and then approached the throne of the Queen of Heaven.

St. Michael, saluting her with great reverence, said: "Hail to thee, Mary Most Holy, Daughter of God the Father."

St Gabriel said: "Hail to Thee, Mary Most Holy, Mother of God the Son."

St. Raphael said: "Hail to thee, Mary Most Holy, Most Pure Spouse of the Holy Ghost."

Then, joined by all the celestial hosts, they intoned together: "Hail to Thee, Mary Most Holy, Temple and Sacrarium of the Most Holy Trinity."

In an instant, like a flash of lightning, this august trio was in the choir. They were joined by the Seraphic Father, St. Francis. From his wounded hands issued celestial rays, which penetrated the heart of Mother Mariana and transported it with love of God and His Holy Mother. Accompanied by all the celestial hosts, St. Francis and the three Archangels approached the unfinished statue. In what seemed to Mother Mariana but an instant, they had transformed it.

Then St. Francis took the white cord that he wore around his waist, and placed it on the holy statue. With love and reverence, he said: "My Lady, I entrust to thy maternal love my sons and daughters of the three Orders that I founded while I was a pilgrim on earth. I deliver to you today and for always this Convent built upon my labors. Difficult times of barrenness and spiritual hunger will come over it, with my sons withdrawing from it for a long period of time. During this time, thou will be the consolation for my daughters who will live here. There will be illegitimate daughters also, alas! but they will be happy only in appearance, for in their depths, they will lack virtue. These will become sharp tools to chisel and polish my true daughters. For the latter, I give my blessing and ask thy support. But for the others, final justice!"

With this, the statue became illuminated, as if engulfed by the sun itself. The Holy Trinity gazed upon it with pleasure and the angels sang the *Salve Sancta Parens*. The Queen of Heaven herself then approached the statue and entered into it like the rays of sun penetrate beautiful crystals. At that moment the holy statue took on life and sang with a celestial voice the *Magnificat*. This took place at three in the morning on January 16, 1611.

"Woe to Lapsed Religious of the 20th Century!"

Mother Mariana then saw her aunt and Founding Mother of the Royal Convent of the Immaculate Conception in Quito, Mother Maria de Jesus Taboada. Mother Maria gazed upon the statue with great love and reverence, and afterward turned her eyes upon her niece. "My daughter," she said. "I congratulate you for the great graces that Divine Goodness now concedes to you and to my Convent. Throughout this ill-fated time of separation from the Friars Minor, this support will be needed to insure the life of this Convent, founded by me at the cost of great labor and sacrifices, as you know well. Centuries will pass before the Friars Minor will again have jurisdiction over it. Until this day comes, my good and faithful daughters will taste the bread of much bitterness and tears. All these, I recognize and bless. Their names are written on the Hearts of God, Mary Most Holy, and my own."

Then she spoke of the many illegitimate daughters who would pretend to great virtue who would also inhabit these cloisters. Madre Taboada said: "Woe to those of the 20th century. Deserting the ranks under the pretext of its excessive rigor, they will want to discontinue the observation of the Rule of Julian II, under which I founded my Convent. Even before that, they will have abandoned the early morning Little Office and other holy practices, which are the support of the spiritual life.[15]

"I repeat: Woe to those who will cause these things to come about! They will tremble before the dreaded judgment seat of God, Who only acknowledges the persevering and militant practice of solid virtue, acquired by dint of relentless battle, fought under the most holy gaze of God .... Moreover, great calamities will befall the people of this epoch. The prayers of the faithful religious will be powerful in holding back the arm of Divine Justice."

It was already 3:30 a.m., the time that Mother Mariana normally went to the dormitory to call the Community to rise and pray the Little Office. Mother Maria de Jesus Taboada told

---

[15] Since we are already living in the 21st century, it seems evident that this vision is describing the crisis that took place in religious life after Vatican II. Applying the principles of the documents issued by Vatican II and subsequent related documents calling for "updating" religious life, almost all the Orders abandoned or reformed their prior Rules, under the pretext of an excessive rigor. Religious habits, discipline, and community life were done away with or radically liberalized. The result of this "opening to the modern world" among women Religious has been the unraveling of Orders and a severe drought for new vocations. Ann Carey, *Sisters in Crisis: The Tragic Unraveling of Women's Religious Communities,* (Huntington, IN: Our Sunday Visitor Publishing House, 1997).

her niece to make haste to call her sisters as was her custom. Mother Mariana immediately returned to her senses and saw before her the beautiful sacred statue, emanating light as if it were engulfed by the sun.

The Community Sees the Completed Statue

Mother Mariana hastened to obey. She told the community nothing of what had happened, but as they climbed the steps to the choir to pray the Little Office, all heard the angelic voices intoning the *Salve Sancta Parens*. They hastened their steps and found the whole choir enveloped in a celestial light. The Holy Image had been transformed. It was no longer a work made by human hands, but a masterpiece remade by the Angels.

From the face of Our Lady issued rays of bright light that diffused themselves throughout the choir and church. Little by little, the light became less brilliant so that the sisters could draw near and contemplate the miracle worked by God for His Convent, and for mankind in general. The physiognomy of the holy statue was majestic, but not severe. On the contrary, it was serene, sweet, amiable, and attracting, as if she were inviting her daughters to approach with confidence their Heavenly Mother. It is impossible to find a picture that does justice to this image, whose skin tone radiates a warmth and life as if it were real, and whose bearing and expression is at the same time so royal and so maternal.

The Divine Child was a masterwork, whose countenance expressed love and tenderness for His humble spouses. One of the first things one notes about the present statue of the Christ Child that appears in the left arm of Our Lady is that it seems of an inferior quality. The skin seems dull and lifeless next to that of Our Lady, the features much less expressive.

In fact, this statue is not the original one, made by the Angels, but a replacement made by men. During a revolution in the 19th century, one of the sisters hid the original Divine Child in one of the convent walls to safeguard it. The sister died unexpectedly, without revealing where she had placed the miraculous image. Mother Mariana had foreseen this event, but she also had predicted that the statue would be found in a miraculous, and not human, way. This would be after the Friars Minor had returned to govern the Convent and Our Lady had intervened in a fortuitous way in History. It can appear to the viewer that Our Lady herself is awaiting the happy day of the restoration not only of her Only Begotten Son but also of Holy Mother Church.

The Sculptor's Testimony

At the agreed upon hour, Francisco del Castillo arrived at the Convent with the special paints he had procured to make the final touches to his masterpiece. Mother Mariana and the Founding Mothers had agreed that they would say nothing to the sculptor about the transformation.

When he arrived at the upper choir, he froze in astonishment and exclaimed with great emotion: "Mother, how can this be? This magnificent statue is not my work! I cannot express what my heart feels! This is an angelic work, for a work of this nature could not be created on this earth by the hands of a mere mortal. No sculptor, no matter how skilled he might be, could ever render such perfection and such unearthly beauty!"

He fell to his knees before the feet of the holy image as tears poured from his eyes. For thus are truly Catholic souls moved in face of the marvels and grandeur of God.

Finally, he rose. Immediately he asked for paper and ink so that he might draw up a written testimony. In it he swore that this blessed statue was not his work, but that of the Angels. He testified that he had left the statue in the upper choir six days earlier with the intention of returning on this day, the 16th of January in the year 1611, to give it the final coat of paint that it lacked. But, he wrote, never in all of his 67 years of life had he seen – neither in the New World nor in Spain – a skin tone comparable to that of the miraculous and blessed statue.

The Bishop Confirms the Miracle

Deeply moved, Francisco del Castillo left the Convent and hurried to the house of Bishop Salvador de Ribera. He lost no time in recounting all that happened, including his written testimony of the miracle, a document that he had left in the privileged Convent as a record for men of all centuries.

Eager to see such a transformation with his own eyes, the Bishop rose and asked the sculptor to accompany him to the Convent of the Immaculate Conception. The door opened quickly to the Prelate, who, accompanied only by the sculptor, entered the upper choir. There he found the statue miraculously changed, just as the sculptor had described. It was much more perfect and beautiful than anything he could have imagined.

Falling to his knees before it, he cried out to Mary, the Mother of Grace and Mercy, begging that she grant him a longer time on earth, for he felt great need of it.

When he rose, he asked to meet with Mother Mariana in the confessional.

"My Life Will Become Known in the 20th Century"

Mother Mariana de Jesus Torres presented herself in the confessional with her customary docility and simplicity. The Bishop demanded to know all that occurred with regard to the miraculous change in the statue. Without hesitation, Mother Mariana recounted all the marvelous things that had taken place in those blessed hours of the early morning of January 16th.

She told the Bishop that she had also been given to know that the testimony of the sculptor, as well as various other precious things, including the statue of the Divine Child, would be hidden by her successors in a closet inlaid in some wall in the Convent because of the public outbreaks of war during the time when the Colony would be making itself a free Republic. "They will do this," she forewarned, "because they will fear the loss of these precious articles. They will not have the light to understand that no earthly power can cause harm to this Convent."

She noted, however, that this would be the will of God, for even her life would not become known until the 20th century. The statue of the Divine Infant would be found when the Friars Minor returned, but this would not take place until humble violence was made to Heaven with pleas for its recovery. No mere human recourse would be sufficient to discover it.

The Bishop listened to the account with great emotion. "Why does Your Reverence say that your life will be written and become known in the 20th century?" he asked.

"Because my person and name are inseparable from the apparition of Our Lady of Good Success," Mother Mariana de Jesus Torres answered. "All this will be recorded in order to verify its truth to those times that will be so decadent in faith. At the present time it is not desirable to reveal any of this because of the propensity of the people to idolatry."

"Mother," the Bishop added, "I seem to have heard you say that this Colony will become independent from Spain and become a free Republic. How can this be?"

"Your Excellency, this will occur after two centuries. It will not take place in our time. We will witness it from Heaven."

"Mother, if it is necessary for the Friars Minor to return to care for this Convent, how can I be of assistance? For this would be virtually impossible now due to the present critical circumstances."

Mother Mariana counseled him not to be concerned, for this would happen only much later. For now, she warned him, it would suffice for him to prepare for his death.

Hearing this, the Bishop started, "Mother, can you not ask God to prolong my time yet a while longer?"

"It is late for this," Mother Mariana said kindly, "for the day and hour of ending our mortal course is fixed for each one of us. Moreover, it is better to die than to live."

The Novena and Consecration of the Holy Statue

The Bishop told Mother Mariana that preparations should begin for the consecration of the statue. Friars and priests from all the monasteries, as well as the general public, should be invited, although they would not be told about the miraculous and merciful intervention of Heaven in the event. He instructed the Convent to make a novena of preparation, which would begin on January 24 and end on February 2, a pious devotion that is still practiced every year in the Convent to this day. The solemn consecration at which the Bishop would officiate and the Marquesa would stand as godmother would take place on the last day, the feast of the Purification of the Blessed Virgin Mary, or Candlemas. This day remains one of special celebration, the Convent's feast day, one might say, for it was on this day that Our Lady gave so many special favors and blessings to the Royal Monastery of the Immaculate Conception and her favored daughter Mother Mariana de Jesus Torres.[16]

On February 2, 1611, all the sisters rose at early dawn to recite the Little Office and to prepare themselves to receive the beautiful statue Our Lady had given them. The Bishop, for his part, had called together the entire Episcopal Chapter and the Royal Assembly to assist at this solemn public ceremony. At 9 a.m., the hour scheduled for the ceremony to begin, the church was overflowing with people of every age and state of life. The Marquesa, occupying a place of honor as godmother, was dressed with the greatest gala and appeared almost royal. As godmother, she was permitted to stand on the lower altar during the ceremony.

---

[16] Many of the most important prophecies of Our Lady of Good Success were made to Mother Mariana on February 2, the Feast of the Purification. The most significant apparition for our times took place on February 2, 1634. As Mother Mariana was praying before the altar, the sanctuary light was mysteriously extinguished. Then Our Lady explained the five meanings of this, all of which pertain to the crisis in the Church and society of our times. *Our Lady of Good Success – Prophecies for Our Times*, pp. 54-60.

The statue was carried down from the upper choir and placed on the lower altar, along with the beautiful crosier, the crown, and the brooch. Alongside these were also a beautiful necklace of fine pearls and three gold rings, one with a precious emerald, another with a diamond, and the third finely set with rubies in the form of a small royal crown. These were yet other gifts offered by the Marquesa and had been placed on a small golden shell engraved in letters adorned with emeralds: *I am Mary Most Holy of Good Success, February 2, 1611.*

At the close of the ceremony, the Bishop asked all present to join him in three Hail Marys. After each one all prayed the salutations of the Archangels: *Hail Mary most holy, Daughter of God the Father. Hail Mary most holy, Mother of God the Son. Hail Mary most holy, Spouse of the Holy Ghost. Hail Mary most holy, Temple and Sacrarium of the Most Holy Trinity.* This marked the commencement of the solemn procession through the lower cloisters of the Convent, which ended in the upper choir, where the holy statue was enthroned so that there she might govern the Convent and watch over all mankind.

The people who had accompanied the statue in the procession felt an unusual piety and movement of heart in its presence. At the door of the cloisters, they tried to push forward in order to remain with the holy statue. They were refrained only by the military guard, which was present there to prevent this. However, to calm them, the Bishop reminded the people that every year the statue would be carried to the lower choir for public veneration for nine days before and after February 2.

The Abbess' throne had been prepared in the upper choir just as the Queen of Heaven had requested. The sculptor, Francisco del Castillo, had carved an elaborate golden niche in the wall over the Abbess' chair. In it he had arranged crimson silk and gold tasseled drapery topped by a crown. Here the procession ended, and the Bishop intoned the *Salve Regina*, then sang the invocations of the *Litany of Loreto* while the religious responded. In thanksgiving for the great favor God had granted the Convent, he asked that until the end of time the *Salve Re-*

gina and the *Litany* be sung every Saturday after the Convent Mass.

With tears flowing from his eyes, the Bishop reverently and tenderly placed the crown on the head of the holy statue, saying, "My Lady, I deliver to Thee the Church." Then he placed the crosier in her right hand, saying, "My Lady, I deliver to thee the government of this Convent and of my flock in general." Finally, placing the keys in the hand holding the crosier, he said, "My Lady and my Mother, I deliver to thee my soul. Open to me the doors of Heaven, for the life remaining to me is quite brief. Watch over this altar and this cloister of your daughters with care and affection. Defend it always and preserve in it the religious spirit with which the spouses of thy Most Holy Son should be imbued."

The Community Flourishes and Grows

As the days and months passed, the Community began to grow, with the number of vocations multiplying so rapidly that the Bishop was forced to suspend admission of novices until the death of an older sister left an opening.

During this period all the religious were most fervent, and they strove to make their least action reflect a great love for God, their Heavenly Mother and their holy Abbess, whose example of solid and heroic virtue all without exception imitated. Thus they made themselves pleasing to their Creator, Who desires such truly holy souls for His cloisters so that they might placate His ire for the many crimes committed in the world. The great secret that would assure religious of the love of God and His Blessed Mother, Mother Mariana often instructed her daughters, was the practice of humility, regular observance of the Rule, and secret sacrifices and penances. These would be for all time the safeguards for those who would progress in the supernatural life.

The Prophecy Fulfilled

As for the Bishop, everything happened exactly as had been foretold. Soon after he had blessed the statue of Our Lady of Good Success, Bishop Salvador de Ribera died unexpectedly on the night of March 24, 1612. Some minor carelessness brought on a severe case of pneumonia, which caused his death. According to the account she later made to her spiritual director, Mother Mariana de Jesus Torres found herself at the deathbed of Bishop Ribera. She was accompanied by the Queen of Heaven, who, in return for the devotion that he had showed to her holy image, had now come to help him in his final anguish. In her blessed hand she carried the keys that the Bishop had offered to Her one year before his death.

And while the little people of Quito soon forgot the Bishop, whom they neither loved nor mourned, Mother Mariana did not forget the imprudent Prelate. Until her death in 1635, she prayed and did penance for his soul so that his purgatory might be shortened and less severe.

* * *

"NO PUDE HACER MAS POR TI PARA MOSTRARTE MI AMOR"

The statue of the Child Jesus Crucified on Pichincha Mountain sets on a side altar in the Conceptionist Church. The devotion has been approved by the Church since the 17th century.

Chapter VI

THE CHILD JESUS OF THE CROSS ON PICHINCHA MOUNTAIN

Another beautiful statue stands on a side altar of the Church of the Immaculate Conception in Quito. Like the statue of Our Lady of Good Success, its origin was unknown for many years. Like the statue of Our Lady of Good Success, Our Lady had commanded Mother Mariana de Jesus Torres to have this image of the Child Jesus made exactly as He appeared to her upon the Pichincha Mountain, a volcanic mountain still active today that towers over the city of Quito.[17]

The vision of the Christ Child Crucified on Mount Pichincha in 1628 reveals the origin of a popular Spanish devotion. Christ, who appears as a child or adolescent in the various holy cards depicting the scene, embraces the Cross in anticipation of His future sacrifice and asks mankind this poignant question: "How can I do more to show My love for you?"

This devotion finds deep roots in Catholic tradition. In *The City of God,* Blessed Mary of Agreda tells us that when Our Lord was still a youth in the house of Nazareth, He would often assume a position in the form of a cross. In the presence of His Mother, who would then imitate His prayers and position, He would pray: "O most blessed Cross! When shall thy arms receive Mine? When shall I rest on thee and when shall My arms, nailed to thine, be spread to welcome all sinners?" (*The Trans-fixion*). The apparition of the Child Jesus Crucified on Mount Pichincha, which Our Lady promised Mother Mariana was des-

---

[17] The Pichincha Mountain overlooks the city of Quito at a distance of about seven miles. Serene and pacific to all appearances, Pichincha is a volcano, the site of 25 historic eruptions, a kind of symbol, it would seem, of the volatile history of the small Central American country favored by Heaven with so many miracles, wonders, and saints. In 1993 the volcano once again became active after 339 years of dormancy.

tined to do a great good for souls, presents a vivid and moving picture of the Christ Child's great love for the sons and daughters of Adam and His great desire – even in His delicate youth – to suffer for their redemption.

The End of the Beautiful Dawns

Toward the end of 1628, Mother Mariana was praying at midnight in the upper choir when Our Lord revealed to her many of the future events of the Spanish Colony. She saw the whole Colony in agitation, a war of independence, and the land bathed in blood. Her heart felt that it would break upon seeing all this chaos and destruction, and she begged Our Lord that His will might prevail and that the party He favored might triumph.

She then understood that the Colony would separate itself from its mother country and become a Republic. This would be a chastisement for the infidelities and innumerable abuses of so many of the authorities sent by the King to govern the Colony.

She saw that when this would happen, the beautiful dawn that each morning would break forth with refulgence over this land – so enchantingly spectacular that some persons would rise at daybreak just to see the day break – would lose some of its brilliance. Thus does earth reflect Heaven, and the earth's beauty and vitality diminish with sin and infidelity to grace. This favor of the beautiful dawns would cease, Mother Mariana was given to understand, because the Republic would become corrupt and ungrateful for the benefits it received from God.

She saw that not only civil, but also ecclesiastical offices would be held by numerous obdurate and malicious Judases. Instigated and possessed by the diabolic spirit, they would sell their Lord for a few coins. She saw the miserable and disastrous fate of these poor souls for all eternity.

The secret as well as public chastisements that this poor Colony, which would then be called the Republic of Ecuador, were revealed to her. She was given to know that the Republic would have been destroyed and buried under the debris of an earthquake if the Divine Goodness had not raised up heroic and just souls in secret and diverse ways. These souls were the victims who would placate Divine Justice with their prayers, sacrifices, and great sufferings during this sad epoch.

War Between the Angels and the Devils

After witnessing the end of the war, she saw Ecuador completely covered by a black cloud composed of countless demons. With diabolical screams and laughter, they tried to overpower the new Republic so that they might govern from its very inception. For its foundation, they laid the malice of the seven capital sins and hatred of Our Lord and His Blessed Mother. They tried to abolish all the convents, cloisters, and pious institutions. Thus they breathed their blasphemous fumes throughout the land, polluting the whole atmosphere with a dense fog that obscured the precious light of faith in souls and hardened the hearts of the people.

In the next vision, Heaven opened its skies and a clear strong light streamed over all of Ecuador. From every convent and cloister issued a cloud of stars that rose to Heaven, and she heard the voice of the Prince of Angels, St. Michael, say: "Descend immediately to the depths of the abyss, cursed black legions, for here God lives, God triumphs, and God reigns in all times by means of His chosen souls! The more triumphant you think yourselves to be, the nearer approaches your defeat! Woe to this new Republic without its religious communities! For without them, it could not subsist!"

Then lightning flashes and swords of fire pierced every corner of the land. The diabolical legions fled, but howled their threats to wage a cruel war unceasingly against this small portion of the earth, where the Woman, their enemy, would be so venerated and loved. For, they screamed in their fury, if they could only succeed in extinguishing the people's devotion to Her, the victory would be theirs. "The time will come," they cried, "when we will have excellent agents who will conquer almost all of this land for us. We will reward them with earthly pleasures, comforts, and riches, and then we will torment them in Hell for all eternity because these ungrateful wretches ignored the mercies and benefits of their Creator." As the demons were expelled, a great calm returned and the sun shone with a tremendous brilliance.

Vision of the Child Jesus on the Pichincha Mountain

Then Our Lady of Good Success carrying her Divine Infant in her right arm appeared to Mother Mariana and said: "Lift your eyes now and look at the Pichincha Mountain, where you will see this Divine Infant, Whom I carry in my arms, crucified. I deliver Him to the Cross so that He might always give good successes to this Republic."

The Archangels Michael, Gabriel, and Raphael carried the Divine Child to Pichincha Mountain. There, surrounded only by thorn bushes bearing a delicate flower, the Child Jesus took the form of child of about 12 to 15 years of age. His expression sweetly majestic, He prostrated Himself on the ground with His arms in a cross and prayed to His Eternal Father to look with favor on Ecuador.

A celestial light enveloped the whole mountain, and the Christ Child rose and stood before a cross with the inscription INRI at its top. On the left arm of the cross hung a crown of sharp thorns; on its right, a white stole. The three Archangels reappeared, with St. Gabriel carrying a white Host, St. Michael bearing a long white tunic speckled with stars, and St. Raphael carrying a mantle of a magnificent rose color unknown on this earth.

The Child Jesus vested Himself in the white tunic and stole, and draped the magnificent mantle over them. Having done this, Christ approached the cross, took the crown of thorns and placed it on His head. He then extended His arms and remained crucified. The Sacred Wounds appeared, but there was no sign of any nails on His hands or feet. Down His cheeks streamed large tears, which were gathered up by the Archangels

St. Michael and St. Raphael and dispersed throughout the new nation.

He then ordered St. Gabriel to place the Host behind His head, where it became a kind of halo behind the Christ Child. Three resplendent beams of light streamed from it. On the center ray appeared the word **love**, on the ray to His right, **Ecuador**, and on the ray to His left, **Spain**. His expression reflected an intense pain, but also a serene joy to suffer for those whom He loved so dearly.

As drops of blood fell from the wounds on His hands, feet, and forehead, He fixed His gaze on the country and said these words: "I can do no more to show My love for you. Ungrateful souls, who repay the great love and attentions of My Heart with contempt, sacrileges, and blasphemies. At least you, My beloved and hidden spouses, be My consolation in My eucharistic solitude. Keep watch in My Company. Do not be overcome by the sleep of indifference to God, Who loves you so much. Always be the heroines of your country during the bitter and dire times that will come. Your humble, secret, and silent prayer and voluntary penances will save it from the destruction toward which its ungrateful sons will lead it. For these wretched ones, rejecting and despising the good, will exalt and serve the evil and self-serving minions of Satan."

Thus was the Child Jesus crucified on Pichincha Mountain.

Six Years Later: Another Vision

In 1634, one year before her death, Mother Mariana de Jesus Torres received another vision of Our Lady of Good Success, who appeared as always with the Child Jesus in her left arm and crosier in her right hand. Once again, she spoke of the war that was coming where the Colony would separate itself from the Spanish Kingdom to become a free Republic. To comfort her daughter in her great grief over the knowledge of this severance, the Queen of Heaven consoled her with these words:

"I will have you know that this severance is desired by God, for this will diminish the responsibilities of the Monarchs, who have appointed their representatives to govern this land. For these representatives who become ambitious and arrogate undue liberties offend the Church, insult the Ministers of God, and consider themselves to be absolute masters over everything.

"You know of the countless evils that will be inflicted upon the Church in this Colony during these times, even by its ecclesiastic representatives, also appointed through the favor of the Kings. Because of this, how many scandals will be given! How many disputes and quarrels will arise! How many sins will be committed that will offend God!

"But We have a great love for this small portion of earth, which will one day be Ecuador. Taking into account the truly good souls who will live here, We pledge that one day as a Republic it will be solemnly consecrated to the Most Sacred Heart of My Divine Son. Then, with a loud voice will it be proclaimed from one end of the country to the other: The Republic of the Sacred Heart of Jesus."

The Mysterious Prophecy Repeated

Then Our Lady repeated the mysterious prophecy that she had given in the great apparition of February 2, 1634, when the tabernacle light had been extinguished. [18] This prophecy seems to apply to the great crisis that the Church has suffered as a consequence of Vatican II. She said: "Dire times will come, during which even those who should justly defend the rights of the Church will be blinded. Without any problem of conscience, these bad Shepherds will instead assist the enemies of the Church or help them accomplish their designs.

"But woe to the error of the wise, to he who governs the Church, the Pastor of the flock that My Most Holy Son confided into his care. And when they appear triumphant and when the authority abuses my power, committing injustices and oppress-

---

[18] *Our Lady of Good Success – Prophecies for Our Times*, pp. 62-38.

ing the weak, near will be their downfall. Dumbfounded, they will fall to the ground."

Our Lady continued, referring to the restoration of the Holy Church "Then, joyful and triumphant, like a tender child, the Church will be reborn and will sweetly sleep, cradled in the capable arms and maternal heart of my most beloved elect son of those times, who will render himself docile to the inspirations of grace. We will fill him with graces and very special gifts; We will make him great on earth and even greater in Heaven, where We have reserved for him a most precious seat. For, without fear of man, he fought for the truth and dauntlessly defended the rights of the Church, for which he will justly be called a martyr."

Our Lady Orders Pictures to Be Made of the Christ Child of Pichincha

"You saw my Divine Child crucified on Pichincha Mountain," Our Lady continued. "This was not by mere chance. Since this mountain dominates the city, my Most Holy Son wants to sanctify this place, where the Sacred Heart of My Jesus wants to exercise His dominion.

"And just as, by my command, my statue will remain upon the Abbess' seat in the upper choir of this Convent to govern and defend it as well as for the well-being of the whole country, so also do We desire that you have pictures made of this vision. For this, you should avail yourself of the present Bishop, a prudent and virtuous Prelate who governs with great meekness of heart. On these pictures should be written the very words that you heard from the lips of your Crucified Love on Pichincha Mountain ["I can do no more to show My love for you"]. These pictures will travel throughout the whole world and will be the source of holy inspirations, but their origin will not be known for some time. The day will come, however, when it will be known."

At the same time of this vision, Our Lady enlightened the heart of Bishop Pedro de Oviedo, a truly good and holy

Prelate, who was permitted to contemplate the scene of the Child Jesus on the cross on Pichincha Mountain. Thus, when Mother Mariana approached him with the request that the pictures be made, the Bishop acceded. He ordered the pictures to be made in Spain with the firm conviction that the devotion would spread and would have the grace of winning hearts to the love of God.

Mother Mariana also had a statue sculpted of the Divine Child exactly as she had seen Him on Pichincha Mountain. With the permission of the ecclesiastical authority, it was introduced for the veneration of the faithful under the invocation of the Child Jesus of the Cross of Pichincha. This devotion has continued to our time, and the statue stands on a side altar for public veneration in the Church of the Immaculate Conception Convent.

Prophecies Fulfilled

Time has borne witness to the truth of the prophecies of Our Lady regarding the Spanish Colony that became the Republic of Ecuador. The move for independence was hastened by Napoleon's armed invasion of the Iberian Peninsula in 1807-8 and his disruption of monarchical rule by taking prisoner King Ferdinand VII of Spain. Thus, almost two hundred years to the day, on May 13, 1830, authorities of Quito proclaimed Ecuador to be a "free and independent State." The decisive battle on Mount Pichincha in 1822 that set Ecuador on its path to independence took place at the very site where the Christ Child appeared crucified to Mother Mariana in 1628.

Civil wars and political unrest followed on the heels of the war of independence in the new Republic of Ecuador. From the beginning Freemasons sought control of the government. The anti-clerical and anti-aristocratic forces lined up with the first president, Juan Flores, a Mason, against the religious and political conservatives.[19] At the same time, ecclesiastical abuses were flagrant, with concubinage, profligacy, gambling and the open violation of monastic rules scandalously common among the Ecuadorian clergy, just as Our Lady of Good Success had forewarned.

But Ecuador also had the great consolation of having the "truly Catholic" president promised by Our Lady to Mother Mariana.[20] In 1860 Gabriel Garcia Moreno (1821-1875) was elected president. Welding an alliance with the Church, he instituted a strict reform under conservative policies and brought a period of stability and prosperity to Ecuador. The 1861 Constitution written under his guidance established Catholicism as the state religion. He reformed and disciplined monks and priests and turned the educational system over to them. A subsequent constitution promulgated in 1869 further infuriated the liberals by excluding heretics from citizenship. In 1873 he consecrated Ecuador to the Sacred Heart of Jesus, as foretold to Mother Mariana more than 200 years earlier.

On August 6, 1875 as he prepared for a third term, Garcia Moreno was assassinated by the Masons out of hatred for the Catholic Faith, in whose defense he had employed an intransigent militancy. His brutal murder precipitated Ecuador into a period of new conflicts and instability that stretched into the 20th century.

Significance of the Vision: Youth Was Made for Sacrifice, Not Pleasure

The vision of the Christ Child Crucified has a particular meaning for our times. As Mother Mariana confided to Bishop Oviedo, "All this will be recorded now in order to verify its truth in those times [the 20th century] that will be so decadent in faith."

---

[19] Mark van Aken, *King of the Night: Juan José Flores and Ecuador 1824-1864* (Berkeley: University of California Press, 1989), pp. 8-11.
[20] M. Horvat, *Our Lady of Good Success*, p. 37.

The Christ Child on the Cross of the Pichincha presents a poignant picture of Our Lord as an adolescent embracing the Cross in His love for mankind – and an example for those who would follow in His footsteps. Our modern age has been preaching the exact opposite to youth throughout the 20th century: Youth was made for pleasure. Have a good time! You are only young once! This devotion encourages young people to the exact opposite: to sacrifice oneself for the great causes, to embrace the Cross, and to renounce the pleasures of this life, even legitimate ones, in preparation for eternity. It is an invitation to be serious about life, for it is only in life that one achieves his place in the glory of Heaven, or for the sake of brief earthly pleasures and honors, falls into eternal damnation.

The Accuracy of Past Prophecies Gives Assurance of Future Promises

Events in Ecuador came to pass exactly as Our Lady of Good Success prophesied to Mother Mariana: the Republic was proclaimed 200 years after the vision. Masonic forces tried to control it from its very inception. A truly Catholic president dedicated the Republic to the Sacred Heart of Jesus. The devils have besieged this morsel of land so beloved by Our Lord and Our Lady with political chaos and anti-clerical schemes.

The perfect accuracy of these prophecies, as well as so many others, lends support and credibility to those that are still to be fulfilled.

For Our Lady has also predicted a great victory, not only for Ecuador but for the whole world. At the very moment when "the evil will appear triumphant and when the authority abuses my power," this would "mark the arrival of my hour, when I, in a marvelous way will dethrone the proud and accursed Satan, trampling him under my feet and fettering him in the infernal abyss."[21]

---

[21] Ibid., p. 18, p. 58.

Her statue, a miraculous work completed by St. Francis and the Archangels Michael, Gabriel, and Raphael, exudes a sweet serenity and encourages confidence in this great promise of a victory. One senses an immense goodness in her gaze, which communicates a grace that whispers in the depth of the soul that we need only confide, and she will give everything. Confiding in that maternal goodness, we can turn to Our Lady of Good Success certain that she will come to our assistance in our personal trials and sufferings because she is our Mother. And she will come to the aid of the Holy Church, the Mystical Bride of Christ, in this terrible crisis because she is Queen of Heaven and Earth. It is this promise that yet remains to be fulfilled.

*   *   *

OUR LADY
OF GOOD SUCCESS
- PROPHECIES FOR OUR TIMES -
Marian Therese Horvat, Ph.D.
Foreword by Atila Sinke Guimarães

Our Lady of Good Success – Prophecies for Our Times relates in detail many of the most important prophecies concerning our times that Our Lady made to Mother Mariana.

It is available for $7 (plus $3 shipping) from TIA, Inc. PO Box 23135, Los Angeles, CA 90023.

Chapter VII

MOTHER MARIANA AND THE QUARRELING FAMILIES

The last years of Mother Mariana de Jesus Torres' life were filled with many new visions and miracles, all of which seem to have application in a metaphorical sense to our times. In particular, the story of her mediation between two quarreling families of Quito seems to have a special significance today, when quarrels and disagreements divide so many of the faithful who are fighting for Holy Mother Church. In both the secular and spiritual spheres, petty arguments and unreasonable angers prohibit the good from uniting in a common fight against the real evil, the progressivism that has infiltrated even into the City of God, as foreseen by Our Lady of Good Success .

For this reason, it seemed opportune to conclude with this narration. The story illustrates the constant plotting of the demons, who strive to cause division among the good. At the same time, it shows the importance of prayer, sacrifice, and recourse to Our Lady as weapons in the sphere of the supernatural, the higher and more important reality.

The story offers an interesting parallel with the Holy Passion of Our Lord. At the command of Our Lady, the demons were hurled into the abyss at the moment of the Crucifixion so that they might be hindered in their conspiring against the nascent Church. At the command of Mother Mariana de Jesus Torres, the demons tormenting the two warring families were flung into the earth, causing the ground to quake and tremble. Without doubt, at the intercession once again of Our Lady in the near future, the demons that were released to inflict so much damage on the Holy Church in the 20th century will once again be hurled, wailing and cursing, into the deep abyss. There at the command of the Virgin Mary they will remain enchained so that, with the torrent of graces that will flow upon a chastised world, the faithful will breathe once again a purer and less infested air and the spirit of religion will prosper in a true Reign of Mary.[22]

The Hours Lengthen Miraculously for Mother Mariana

During the last months of Mother Mariana de Jesus Torres' life, her virtue shone, so to speak, through the walls of her beloved cloister. The people of Quito flocked to her continuously, pleading with insistence to speak to the "Holy Foundress," as she was known.

From the beginning of his office, Bishop Pedro de Oviedo had recognized the great virtue of the last remaining Founding Mother, whose life seemed more that of an angel than a mere human. He used to speak with her almost daily in the confessional to present various problems so that he might discern the will of God by means of this favored soul. Thus, as her days reached their end, she took the opportunity to ask his permission to attend to the many poor and needy persons who desired to speak with her during the intervals between Community acts.

His permission was given, and after this, in her free hours Mother Mariana would receive persons from all the social classes who came to seek her. She used to receive a large number of people in a short period of time, without ever interrupting or disturbing her life in the community. All who visited her would leave tranquil and content. Moreover, great conversions took place because of her words and prayers.

How valuable are the sweet and insistent words of a religious to persons in the world! In her last will and testament, Mother Mariana, counseling her daughters, told them that many souls return to Our Lord after reflecting on words from the lips of His faithful spouses, words to which God gives special unc-

---

[22] The Reign of Mary was predicted by the great Marian Doctor of the 19th century, St. Louis Marie Grignion de Montfort, who foresaw a glorious victory on earth that would establish the Kingship of Christ through Mary for a long period of time. Our Lady confirmed this victory at Fatima in 1917: "In the end, my Immaculate Heart will triumph."

tion, especially when they are accompanied by prayers and sacrifices.

The Bishop Asks a Favor

At this time two leading families of the colonial city
were quarreling over a personal misunderstanding, and each
head-of-family had sworn to take the life of the other. The good
Bishop had exhausted every recourse of prudence, kindness, and
even severity to resolve the conflict. Gravely concerned at the
state of souls of the families, who had ceased to make their
Easter duty, and at the scandal that they were giving to the city,
the Bishop asked Mother Mariana to intercede and meet the two
families separately in the parlor. For he was convinced that Our
Lord would deny none of Mother Mariana's last requests on
earth and that only she could negotiate a truce. She readily
agreed, and the appointments were made.

At the designated hour, the first family, Don Miguel,
Doña Francisca, and their children arrived. The problem was
that a horse and two head of oxen of the second family had died
on Don Miguel's farm. Although it happened due to the negli-
gence of the servants of both parties, each family refused to ad-
mit the guilt of its servants. At the end of his account of this
incident, Don Miguel turned to Mother Mariana and demanded:
"Do you not see how we are right and all the blame lies with
this cursed family, whom we shall never see or speak to again?'

"The language of the true Catholic," returned Mother
Mariana, "that which Our Lord taught us from the Cross on
which He was nailed, was the language of peace, mercy, and
pardon. Every imaginable calumny and injustice and every true
infamy fell upon the Holy of Holies, to the point that this envy,
this hatred, and this scorn delivered Him to crucifixion on the
cross, as if He were a criminal, a murderer, and the most perni-
cious of men. Even the criminal Barrabas was preferred to Him.

"And we, poor creatures, miserable sinners that we are,
how should we deal with the slanders of our fellow men, whose
souls, like ours, were redeemed at the cost of the bitter suffer-

ings of Christ the Redeemer and His Virgin Mother? This vengeance is incompatible with hearts that know God through the precious gift of Faith and the Catholic Religion. It would be excusable, perhaps, among infidels and savages, who do not have even the knowledge of Christ Our Lord."

She asked them to think on this for nine days and for the family to pray together each day an Our Father and a Hail Mary to the Most Holy Virgin of Good Success, the Queen of Peace. The family left, pensive and in a profound silence that weighed over all of its members with a supernatural influence for the rest of the day.

That night, Don Miguel, the most inexorable in the quarrel, called the family together to say the prayers the Holy Foundress had indicated. Upon reaching the words "*Forgive us our trespasses as we forgive those who have trespassed against us,*" no one could finish the prayer. All were prevented from uttering these words, as if by an interior force. Finally, they resolved to pass over the phrase and say the Hail Mary. When they finished, they asked each other in amazement, "What is happening to us? Ah! God, angry with us, justly strikes with His irate Hand!"

That same day Mother Mariana had addressed her sisters before the evening meal and asked them to offer all their prayers and penances for the next nine days to reconcile these two families who were endangering their own souls and giving bad example to the city. "Let us pray together each day three Hail Marys to Our Lady, asking her good success in this matter, and an Our Father to the Holy Ghost, asking that He shed light and grace on these souls. Above all, let us ask that when they pray this prayer taught by Christ Our Lord Himself, upon reaching the words, *forgive us our trespasses as we forgive those who have trespassed against us,* they will feel remorse and divine grace will work in their souls."

The Second Family Tells its Story

The next day, the second family, Don José, Doña Joaquina, and their four children, came to Mother Mariana and said much the same as the first family had the day before. In his fury, Don José went so far as to demand that St. Michael, the family's patron saint, avenge the slanders against them with the death of one of the sick members of the other family. "This will punish them for their pride and presumption," he raged.

Hearing this, Mother Mariana released a long and profound sigh, which penetrated the hearts of all present. Fearing he had scandalized her, Don José insisted, "I spoke thus only to reveal to you what is in my heart. Certainly I would not do this myself, but we are mere creatures and can no longer bear such perverse behavior. If Your Reverence carefully weighs this matter, you will clearly see that we are the offended party."

Mother Mariana replied with great sadness: "What you were thinking did not scandalize me. Rather it buried in my heart a mortal arrow to see Christian charity so fractured and profaned among Catholics and to consider my poor Lord Jesus Christ so despised and abandoned. While He, from the Tabernacle, teaches His beloved sons and daughters to love and pardon their enemies, you speak to Him with quite different words: 'We pay no attention to Thee. We resolve to renew the sufferings of Thy Passion so that we might be satisfied.'

"This is my greatest torment: to consider that a Catholic family would say this by their actions to their Creator. Is this how you would correspond to so many benefits received from the Divine Goodness? I implore you with tears in my eyes to recognize and reconsider your conduct toward Our Lord Jesus Christ. Toward this end, I ask you a favor that you must not deny me."

She then asked that their family also should gather and pray together every evening for nine days an Our Father and a Hail Mary. They agreed and left, certain that God would show that justice was on their side.

First Steps Toward a Reconciliation

At the end of the nine days, the first family hurried to the Convent at the first visiting hour. Don Miguel told Mother Mariana de Jesus Torres how her words had pierced their hearts, and how the family was unable to pronounce the words *forgive us our trespasses*. A fear and panic had come over them upon considering that they would be lying before the God of Truth Who reads all hearts. By saying these words, they realized that they were asking Him to treat them as they were treating their rivals.

"How could we have passed six years and nine months in discord, insults, and hatred – which escalated to the point that we were contemplating murder!" he exclaimed. Now, he was prepared to give not just one horse and two oxen to make peace between the families, but two horses and six head of oxen. However, fearing Don José's implacable anger and hatred, he asked Mother Mariana to arrange a meeting in the parlor so that a formal reconciliation might take place

The next day, the family of Don José came in its turn to speak with Mother Mariana. This patriarch also explained how his family had been unable to pronounce the words asking for forgiveness of their trespasses. They had become convinced that they would never be able to say this prayer so long as they harbored such enmity in their hearts. They had made the resolution to pardon the rival family for the death of the horse and two oxen, and with this, he reported, they had been able to complete the Our Father.

They agreed to meet with Mother Mariana and the other family the very next morning at 10 o'clock in the Convent to make their peace. Joyfully the family took its leave.

A Devil in the Form of a Beggar

On their return home, the family crossed paths with a filthy, weeping beggar who asked for alms. Repulsed by his appearance and way of being, Doña Joaquina turned him away.

But her husband insisted that a charity should be given after receiving such a great grace from God. He took a coin and handed it to the beggar.

The beggar, however, asked to speak a few words aside with him privately. They moved some steps away, and the beggar began to speak earnestly, assuring Don José of his love and devotion. To prove it, the mendicant stated, he would save his life, for only a few hours before, he had heard members of the rival family insulting him in the square and swearing to take his life in the Convent parlor the next day. For they were only pretending to make a peace in order to wreak their vengeance on him and all his family.

The beggar implored Don José neither to go to the Convent nor to place any trust in "that miserable Sister who has no virtue since she had treated him, a poor beggar, with only contempt and scorn." Only that day, he said with tears in his eyes, Mother Mariana had turned him cruelly and sternly away from the Convent. Such uncharitable behavior proved well that she had no real virtue, and only made a pretense of holiness to impress the naïve.

Hearing this, Don José became enraged that such a man would calumniate the Holy Foundress. Raising his cane, he let it fall upon the contemptible beggar. He returned with unease to his family, and they set on their way. But a doubt and disquiet had disturbed the peace and joy of Don José, something that his wife noted immediately. Looking back, she saw the beggar laughing and mocking them. "I fear that loathsome scoundrel," she said to her husband. "His very appearance bodes evil."

When they arrived at their home, Don José, still confused and disturbed, narrated what had taken place. Sensing some great evil boding in the beggar's words and actions, Doña Joaquina immediately set out again for the Convent to ask the counsel of the Holy Foundress. As she narrated the event to Mother Mariana, another visitor burst in. It was Doña Francisca, who cried out in a great flurry of agitation that her family would be the victims of a terrible betrayal. For the same beggar had gone to their house to raise suspicions and re-ignite the fire of hatred there as well.

With the demon's plot thus exposed, the two ladies embraced, the first time in years. With great relief and warmth, they renewed the promise to meet the next morning to complete the reconciliation, which the demon was striving to prevent to frustrate the innumerable graces that would pour down upon both families and to prevent the edification this good example would give to the city.

Universal Mediatrix of Graces

After this Mother Mariana hastened to the Tabernacle to tell Our Lord all that had taken place, as was her custom. As she prayed, she fell into an ecstasy. She saw how the Holy Trinity, in an ineffable and marvelous way, resided in the Consecrated Host in order to be the light of the universe, and how Jesus Christ in the Blessed Sacrament lives a life of impressive activity, unceasingly laboring for the salvation of the souls that had cost Him so dearly. She saw also how the Empress of Heaven took a lively part in all this. For all conversions take place by means of and through the intercession of this Blessed Mother, the necessary channel of divine grace. Jesus Christ always acts through the channel of Mary Most Holy. Christ washes us with His precious Blood; the Holy Ghost inflames us with the fire of divine love, and thus we are presented by Our Lady, cleansed and purified, before God the Father so that He might gaze upon us with mercy and bestow upon us His favors and graces.

Mother Mariana also saw in this revelation the state of souls of the members of the two quarreling families and how near they were walking toward eternal perdition. Furious that their plans had been impeded, the cursed demons were applying all their efforts and infernal shrewdness to try to prevent the reconciliation. Even at that moment, they were engaging in new ruses and intrigues to re-ignite the feud.

Mother Mariana begged Our Lord, by the merits of His Holy Blood and those of the co-Redeemer Mary Most Holy, to impede these new attempts of the demon.

To this plea, Our Lord agreed, responding that He would deny nothing to her, the faithful daughter of His Immaculate Mother, as the days of her earthly exile drew to their end. "You yourself shall command these furious legions of demons who have issued forth to prevent the conversion of these souls to descend to the depths of the infernal abyss," He told her. "Order this in the name of the Mystery of the Holy Trinity, of My Real Presence in the Consecrated Host, and of the Immaculate Conception of My Blessed Mother and her birth. Then see how those foul spirits will flee in panic. And so that you might do this, first see them."

Then she saw an countless number of evil spirits of all shapes, forms, and sizes that were invading the homes of the two families, striving to penetrate their hearts. Among these legions was the loathsome beggar, who had concealed under his coat a long tail covered with thorns, from which he would try to hang the masters of both families.

With great scorn, aversion, and horror, the holy Spanish religious turned her eyes to Our Lord and His Mother, asking that They would assist and accompany her, a poor creature, on such a mission: "Thus escorted and defended by Thy Majesties as Thou hast always appeared to me, I will have good success, hurling these proud and invective spirits into the deep abyss."

The Heavenly Procession Forms

At the conclusion of this plea, Mother Mariana saw the Heavens open and descend into the Sanctuary. The Queen of Heaven approached, followed by the three Archangels, who made a profound bow before the Holy Host in the Tabernacle. St. Michael took the Host in his hands, and the Host became a beautiful Child, Who asked to be placed in the arms of His Mother.

"Now let all of you accompany us," the Christ Child commanded, "so that you might witness the grandeur of the power of God Who makes use of instruments so apparently weak in order to realize great marvels. See, then, the confirmation of that charming truth: God hides His secrets from the proud and great of the world and reveals them to the humble and simple of heart."

St. Michael presented himself before the Sovereign Empress and placed in her left arm her Divine Infant. St. Gabriel approached Our Lady and placed a beautiful crosier in her right hand, saying: "Take, O Lady, in your sovereign hand this crosier, which Divine Omnipotence has placed there so that, as Empress of Heaven and Earth, thou might govern the universe and quash in all times the diabolic force of the tenacious and proud demons, who, filled with envious fury, strive with all their subtle cunning for the perdition of souls. However, they will always be conquered and humiliated by thee, who art the Mother of the Divine Word."

Finally St. Raphael approached, carrying a small but exquisite cross about the size of a finger and embedded with precious jewels. The light that issued from it blinded the eyes of Mother Mariana. The Archangel placed it in the hand of the Divine Infant, and said: "Here, O King of Heaven and Earth, is the gift that Thou dost guard and grant to Thy faithful sons and daughters who serve Thee faithfully during their religious lives. With it, they will triumph over the diabolical scheming. By the Cross will the souls redeemed by Thee be saved." And with a profound bow, the Archangel withdrew.

The whole celestial Court then intoned a hymn of glory whose melody could be relished only by the soul, the bodily senses being unable to support such sweetness without mortally succumbing.

The Apostolate of Religious Souls

When the canticle ended, the Child Jesus directed these words to Mother Mariana:

"My favored spouse, you are a most delicate fiber of My Heart, because you have passed your whole life in My service and you have loved Me with your whole heart and soul, dedicated and untiring in your efforts to conquer souls for Me. In order to convert them, turn them from vice, and direct their steps onto the secure road that leads to Heaven, you have generously and valorously endured great physical and moral sufferings, showing none of that cursed human respect which frustrates the great graces designed for souls and makes them leave off the grand undertakings destined for them. O! If all My spouses were to have this diligence and care in dealing with persons entrusted to them, then how many souls they would secretly give to Me!

"Know that I place in the hands of My spouses double-edged swords to penetrate the most hardened hearts. Even if they appear insignificant, their words resound in the interior of souls night and day, germinating and producing the early or late fruits of penitence. And when such words are accompanied by incessant prayers for these dear sinners, then they are yet more efficacious. I cannot resist the requests of My spouses in their undertakings for the salvation of souls.

"O my predilect daughter! Tell your daughters that they are My apostles from the silence of the cloisters. Assure them that if they do all this, they will have a special glory in Heaven. Affirm that only one word proffered by a religious can weigh most heavily in the hearts of those who live in the world ....

"Now, let us bury in the abyss those cursed legions that have issued from Hell in order to regain these two poor families and thus attempt to rob Me of souls so dear to My Heart."

The Christ Child placed the beautiful cross in the heart of the privileged Mother Mariana as a gift of the eternal nuptials that so soon awaited her. Mother Mariana later told her spiritual director that the divine flames that penetrated the depths of her heart were almost insupportable for her human nature to bear. When she returned to her corporal senses, Our Lord had to mitigate their violence since mere human nature could not have supported it.

Our Lady Speaks of the Contemplative Life

Then the Mother of God spoke to Mother Mariana. She asked her to be even more perfect in the love of God and neighbor in the few days that remained to her in life by increasing her prayers, labors, and sufferings to win souls to God.

"If religious only knew the merit that they gained for eternity in this hidden apostolate," she said, "they would not lose any opportunity. It is a great charity to work, pray, and suffer for these poor wayward souls. Like the prodigal son in the Gospel, such souls abandon the house of their good Father and stray from it by sin. Placing themselves far from God, they thus dissipate their precious inheritance of divine grace until they are reduced to extreme spiritual misery and squalor. Like beggars they live in the world, which is a hard and cruel master, with its acorns of false honors and pleasures, and the husks of pigs, which are the vices and unbridled passions that bury such a great number of souls in Hell, rendering fruitless the Blood and merits of My Redeemer Son .... With the view to re-conquer these prodigal sons, Our Lord established the contemplative life in His Church, so that His chosen souls, hidden from all human eyes, unknown, forgotten, and often despised, would intervene as active and zealous apostles with their incessant prayer and penance in the monastic life.

"Woe to religious souls who, lazy and imprudent, do not carry out their divine mission because of cowardice! They will have no excuse before the Divine Tribunal. There they will be rewarded for the souls they saved, and punished for those who were lost because of their neglect in the vineyard of the Lord.

"Now, let us put to shamed flight the infernal legions who dare to snatch these souls from God."

Victory Over the Infernal Legions

Our Lord and Our Lady, together with all the celestial hosts and the humble Mother Mariana, directed their steps to the infested houses of the two families, where all was confusion, turmoil, and agitation.

Terror-stricken at the appearance of this heavenly procession, the demons wanted to flee, but the angelic Prince St. Michael prevented them.

So also had the cowardly demons acted at the Crucifixion of Our Lord, for when Lucifer and his hosts realized that Christ was the Savior who would vanquish them with His death, they wished to fly and cast themselves into Hell. But at the command of Mary Most Holy, they were forced to go to Calvary and witness the end of the great mysteries there enacted for the salvation of men and the ruin of themselves.[23]

Now, once again, St. Michael commanded the cursed and wretched legions in the name of the Virgin Mary to remain so that their luciferian pride might be humbled by a mere creature.

At the command of the Child Jesus, Mother Mariana fixed the demons with a look of severity and scorn and said: "Evil and repugnant spirits, who because of your luciferian pride fell from Heaven, where the Lord had created you as most beautiful spirits: I, a poor and weak creature who glories in serving my Lord and God, willingly obeying all that He commands of me and loving Him with my whole being, small though it is, I abhor you with the abhorrence with which my God abhors you because of your insubordination.

"And, lamenting that you have vanquished so many souls of God, Who is the one true Lord of all, I thus command you: In the name of the august mystery of the Most Holy Trinity, of the Real Presence of Jesus Christ in the Consecrated

---

[23] Mary of Agreda recounts that the devils were suspicious, but not certain, that Jesus Christ was the Savior until after He had taken up the Cross. Then they tried to flee in panic and despair at their approaching defeat. Mary of Agreda, *The City of God*, The Transfixion, Chap. 23.

Host, and of the mystery of the Immaculate Conception of Mary Most Holy, of whom I have the good fortune to be daughter, and in the name also of her most pure and most integral Virginity and Divine Maternity, she being Virgin Most Pure before, during, and after birth, I command that you depart from these two families, so that they might give glory to His Divine Majesty in the fulfillment of the most holy will of God.

"Descend, then, into the deep pit, your eternal abode. Flee, vanquished by your great ignominy! The Redeeming Cross, which serves as your greatest torment, I bear with pleasure in my heart, for I have been nailed upon it joyfully throughout my life."

With this, she made the Sign of the Cross.

At the same instant, screaming and tearing at each other, the cursed beings hurled themselves into the center of the earth. This caused such a tremor of the ground that the inhabitants of the city became alarmed. Rushing from their homes, they hurried to the churches to beg for mercy, for they thought the Pichincha volcano was erupting and would bury them all.

The two families, however, who had been so irritable and inflamed, immediately became calm. Each family gathered together with all their servants to pray the holy Rosary and a great tranquility and peace descended over them and their households.

The Reconciliation

When morning broke, the two families met as planned at the Convent parlor and were reconciled. Thus, at the end of August 1634, this scandalous and longstanding dispute came to an end. In fact, so great did the friendship remain between the two families that two sons of Don José married two daughters of Don Miguel, to the great happiness of both families.

Henceforth, the two families were examples and models of piety in their frequenting of the Sacraments of Confession and Communion. They asked pardon also of the Bishop for the sufferings they had caused him for not having listened to the voice of their Pastor and Father. Thus they doubly edified the city that had before been so scandalized.

This reconciliation of the two families that had been such terrible enemies caused repercussions throughout the Colony and even outside it. Letters poured in, directed to the humble Conceptionist religious. Seeing so many serious and irresolvable problems and concerns, Mother Mariana felt great compassion and shed many tears. "My God, My God!" she would exclaim to her daughters. "See how such great and numerous afflictions weigh like lead over poor human hearts! O my daughters, how grateful we religious should be to the Divine Goodness, Who has removed us from the tumult of the world and placed us under the shelter of these sacred walls, preserving us from so many bitter problems and heavy responsibilities, which disturb the conscience and place souls in such risk of perdition.

"Here, my daughters, in religious life, what we suffer is nothing in comparison with the difficulties of the world. Moreover, our small sufferings have an immense value before God, while the sorrows suffered in the world have much less. This difference resides in the fact that we have embraced the perfect life, following the evangelical counsels, living and remaining very near to Jesus Christ and occupied only with acquiring merits and virtues for Heaven, the only essential pursuit of true importance.

"Yet those in the world – *pobrecitos* [little poor ones] – even those who are good, are obliged to be distracted by many things, such as acquiring goods to guarantee the future of their children and family, for this is a duty of conscience. Our sublime occupation here is to acquire and lay away riches for our own souls and, consequently, to bequeath good example and solid virtues to our daughters to come, who through the course of time will inhabit these cloisters to be faithful spouses of Our Lord Jesus Christ and victim souls. Uniting themselves with the Eucharistic Victim, they will thus hold back the irate arm of Divine Justice."

At a Command of Our Lady, the Devils Will Be Confounded

Just as the two families were being stirred by the action of the infernal spirits who had infested their homes, the crisis today in the Church and society, predicted by Our Lady of Good Success to Mother Mariana in the 1600's, is not the fruit of mere human action. Man has opened the doors to the devils for them to stimulate, exacerbate, and direct this action of destruction. Logically speaking, the generalized chaos and moral dissolution we are witnessing today could not take place without a preternatural action. Without the cooperation of Lucifer, it would be difficult to imagine that man could arrive at such extremes of pride and sensuality that he is presently reaching.

It is, therefore, crucial to consider the opposition placed between Our Lady and the Serpent since the beginning of time: "*I will place enmities between you and the woman, between your race and her race; she will crush your head and you will lie in wait for her heel*" (Gen 3:15). Given the *imperium*, or power, with which God has invested Our Lady, it is enough that she should give a command for the demons to be confounded and withdraw from the scene of human action. Likewise, it suffices that, for the chastisement of men, she would permit the infernal legions a certain liberty of action for the crisis to reach this extreme of evil we are experiencing today.

Thus we can see how much depends on her rule and dominion. For Our Lord gave Mary Most Holy a royal power over all Creation. He crowned her Queen of the Universe to govern it. Our Lady, united to God in all things and dependent upon Him, nonetheless exercises her action in the lives of men and, therefore, plays a role in the direction of History. Such considerations open the perspectives for the victory, the great heavenly intervention in History at a crucial moment "when all will seem lost." Then, as Our Lady of Good Success told Mother Mariana, she shall return and win the battle against all the powers of evil, and will establish her Reign over the ruins of the gnostic and egalitarian Revolution.

To play our part in this great epopee, the forces of good should put aside all personal interests and petty differences and fight together for the Reign of Our Lord Jesus Christ, with firm confidence that the Sacred Heart of Jesus will reign by means of the wise and Immaculate Heart of Mary, as She promised in Quito in 1634, and again at Fatima in 1917.

* * *

PRAYER TO OUR MOTHER OF GOOD SUCCESS

Soul of Mary, sanctify me,
Body of Mary, purify me,
Heart of Mary, inflame me,
Sorrow of Mary, comfort me,
Tears of Mary, console me,
O Sweet Mary, hear me.
With thy benign eyes, look on me,
Through thy holy steps, guide me,
To thy Divine Son, pray for me,
Pardon for my sins, achieve for me,
Devotion to your holy Rosary, infuse in me,
Love for God and my fellow man, grant me,
Permit me not to ever be separated from thee.
In the hour of my death, comfort me,
From my enemies, defend me,
With the shield of thy holy name, protect me,
With thy mantle, cover me,
In the fatal instant of my agony, assist me,
From dying in sin, free me,
Into the arms of Jesus, deliver me,
To the eternal mansion, bring me,
So that, with the angels and saints
I can praise thee forever and ever, Amen.

From a holy card distributed by the Convent of the Conceptionist
Sisters in Quito.
[With ecclesiastical approval]

TO THE MOST HOLY VIRGIN OF GOOD SUCCESS

Our Lady and Mother, see how evil is invading everything: hearts, families, society, our Country.

Children no longer walk on the path of innocence. The youth, caught up in worldly pastimes, no longer come before thy altar to ask thy maternal blessings; nor do they seek the light of thy gaze to dissipate the shadows of doubt the world instills unceasingly.

Mothers are forgetting that the home is the first school where good is taught, and that they are the first teachers … Family life today has deteriorated, and the sound of the call to prayer is rarely heard.

In the schools there is no prayer, nor are thy grandeurs sung. In the home, few still believe in Holy Providence which has counted all the hairs on our heads and the sufferings of our hearts, and few have recourse to the merciful assistance of thy maternal heart.

In these hours our Country is the poor traveler of the Gospel who fell into the hands of thieves, riddled with wounds that are almost mortal, without the relief of any human hope.

My sweet Mother, take care of these abandoned children who are lost because they have nothing in life. Protect the youth so that these tender plants are not swallowed up in the poisonous muck of vice. Teach mothers the divine gift of being mothers and their duty to model the hearts of their children at the cost of any sacrifice, of saving them with the mysterious supplications of their tears.

If you do not come to the assistance of this agonizing Country, the remnants of Christendom will disappear. Your heart is an abyss of ineffable tenderness. Let a drop of balm fall upon its wounds and it will live. Amen.

From a holy card distributed by the Convent of the Conceptionist Sisters in Quito.

CHRONOLOGY

This chronology cites important dates of events related in two books: *Stories and Miracles of Our Lady of Good Success* and *Our Lady of Good Success – Prophecies for Our Times*

1563: Mariana Francisca de Jesus Torres y Berriochoa Alvarez was born in the province of Biscay, Spain.

Dec. 8, 1572: The First Communion of Mariana at age seven; she received and accepted her vocation.

Dec. 30, 1576: Mother Maria Taboada, the five other Founding Mothers and Mariana de Jesus Torres arrived in Quito after the difficult journey at sea.

Jan. 13, 1577: The Royal Monastery of the Immaculate Conception was founded; The Abbess, Mother Maria de Jesus Taboada, was age 33; her niece Mariana de Jesus Torres was age 13.

Oct. 4, 1579: The solemn profession of Mother Mariana at age 16.

1582: The first death of Mother Mariana, age 19, in which she stood before the Divine Tribunal and chose to return to earth to suffer for 53 more years as an expiatory victim for our times.

Good Friday, 1588: The second death of Mother Mariana, age 25, after she suffered a dark night of the soul where she suffered in both body and spirit.

Oct. 4, 1593: The death of Mother Maria Taboada on the Feast of St. Francis. Mother Mariana was elected Abbess for the first time at age 30.

Feb. 2, 1594: The 1st apparition of Our Lady of Good Success to Mother Mariana. She asked that a statue be made.

Jan. 16 1599:   The 2nd apparition of Our Lady of Good Success. She again commanded that her statue be made and gave the measurement for her height.

1605:   Mother Mariana began the five years of suffering in hell for the soul of the rebellious native sister.

Jan. 20-21, 1610:   The 3rd apparition of Our Lady of Good Success who warned that the making of the statue should not be delayed. Our Lady sent the Archangels to dispel Mother Mariana's doubts and again gave her measurement. She foretold that the Sacraments would be profaned and forgotten in a great crisis in the Church in the 20th century.

Feb. 2, 1610:   The 4th Apparition of Our Lady of Good Success; Our Lady reprimanded Mother Mariana for her fault against obedience and spoke of the need for the statue in the 20th century because of the sins of impurity, blasphemy and heresy.

Feb. 4, 1610:   Mother Mariana spoke to Bishop Ribera, who gave his permission for the statue to be made.

Sept. 15, 1610:   Francisco del Castillo began to sculpt the statue in the upper choir of the Convent.

Sept. 1610:   The Marquesa's arm is cured by the miraculous cord.

Dec. 15, 1610:   Bishop Ribera dreamed about his death and the mercy of Our Lady because he supported the devotion to Our Lady of Good Success.

Jan. 16, 1611:   The Archangels Michael, Gabriel and Raphael, together with St. Francis of Assisi, finished the statue in the upper choir in the early morning.

Jan. 24, 1611:   The first day of the novena of thanksgiving to Our Lady of Good Success.

Feb. 2, 1611:   The Feast of the Purification, or Candlemas. The Statue was christened with holy oils by Bishop Salvador de Ribera, the 8th Bishop of Quito, and placed on the Abbess' chair in the upper choir.

Mar. 24, 1612:   The death of Bishop Ribera.

1619:   Mother Mariana accepted the cross of interior sufferings.

Feb. 2, 1634:   The sanctuary light in the lower choir was extinguished; Our Lady of Good Success explained the five reasons for this, which all pertain to the crisis in the Church and society in the 20th century.

August. 1634:   Mother Mariana resolved the quarrel between the two families. Accompanied by Our Lord, Our Lady and the heavenly hosts, she expelled the demons to the deep abyss.

Dec. 8, 1634:   The last apparition of Our Lady of Good Success with the three Archangels; Our Lady warned about the corruption of customs of priests and religious.

Jan. 16, 1635:   Mother Mariana died at 3 p.m. at age 72.

1906:   The whole and incorrupt body of Mother Mariana was found in the Convent sarcophagus.

August 8, 1986   The Archbishop of Quito issued an Episcopal decree to initiate the Cause of Beatification for the Ven. Mother Mariana de Jesus Torres

Feb. 2, 1991   The canonical coronation of Our Lady of Good Success as Queen of Quito. The same year, the Church of the Conceptionist Convent was declared an Archdiocesan Marian Sanctuary.

*   *   *